twisted

twisted fate

a novel by **norah olson**

KATHERINE TEGEN BOOKS
An Imprint of HarperCollins Publishers

Katherine Tegen Books is an imprint of HarperCollins Publishers.

Twisted Fate
Copyright © 2015 by HarperCollins Publishers

Library of Congress Cataloging-in-Publication Data
Olson, Norah.
    Twisted fate : a novel / by Norah Olson. — First edition.
        pages   cm
    Summary: Told from separate viewpoints, unfolds how sisters
Sydney and Ally Tate's relationship changes as they get involved with
their new neighbor, Graham, an artist with a videocamera who has a
mysterious—and dangerous—past.
    ISBN 978-0-06-227204-1 (hardcover)
    ISBN 978-0-06-238732-5 (int'l ed.)
    [1. Mental illness—Fiction. 2. Sisters—Fiction. 3. Neighbors—
Fiction. 4. High schools—Fiction. 5. Schools—Fiction. 6. Artists—
Fiction.] I. Title.
PZ7.O52155Twi 2015   2014005862
[Fic]—dc23   CIP
                                                  AC

14 15 16 17 18   PC/RRDH   10 9 8 7 6 5 4 3 2 1
❖
First Edition

For Sebastian

twisted fate

SYDNEY

'm not saying that I was right in the end. In fact maybe I'm to blame: the way I was caught off guard; the way I walked out of school that late afternoon with my eyes wide-open, thinking I had a plan, that I could fix everything all by myself, never dreaming how wrong things could go at the harbor.

I had my headphones on and Death Cab for Cutie blasting. I put my board down on the road and skated toward the slips. The autumn air rushed through my hair, and cars whizzed by close enough for me to feel them, and I thought in those moments, giddy and a little high, how I was going to fix things, make everything right in the world. I was going to save us both; protect Ally above everything—even though I could barely stand her half the time, even though we could go for weeks without speaking. But still I was determined to make it all okay. I thought there was no way it could go wrong and so I let myself be happy while I headed to the ocean. And that happiness felt like it was something coming from Ally's head or maybe Ally's heart. And I remember in those moments knowing that we were more alike than I ever could have admitted. Knowing that things between us were different, were finally somehow understood. After all, a sister in many ways is like a second self.

Back before it all happened I felt like one of us must have been adopted. Besides being what our mom breezily calls "pretty" when she takes us all dressed up to one of her fund-raisers or parties, we don't even look alike. Ally has long blond hair that's straight as a board and green eyes and her skin is milky pale and smooth. For as long as I could remember she'd been the good girl, the standard beauty. And I've been her shadow, a photo negative, where all the light spaces, the bright happy spaces, turn to dark. And make no mistake, I am dark. Not just dark thoughts and dark humor. I have dark curly hair, dark eyes, freckles instead of the romantic moonlight-paleness of her face. How we came from the same parents is a complete mystery to me.

If it sounds like I'm jealous of her I'm not. I would not have wanted to live her life or have gone through what she went through in the end. And I'd never in a million years have been naive enough, *stupid* enough, to become friends with Graham Copeland, part skeleton, part zombie in his expensive Diesel jeans, all blond and pretty like Allyson and too stuck up or shy or obsessed with his own weird world to talk to anyone. I could see right away that something wasn't right. The way he looked at her, the way he could never look me in the eye quite the same way.

I remember it so clearly, the day that would change our lives forever: watching the moving van pull out of the driveway of the big old post-and-beam house next door. It was the nicest house in the neighborhood. Rockland is full of these places—mansions actually. Perfect old slate-roofed estates waiting for rich folks to move in. Or weathered stately old gems that people fixed up. Even though it was right next to Graham's, our house was the latter. Rambling and not as square as a place should be. Our dad was a boat builder and he bought it when we were little and fixed it up himself— well, he was still occasionally fixing it up—might be fixing it up forever for all we knew. He was so busy sailing and doing restoration carpentry on other people's mansions that he wasn't around a lot and our house didn't quite get the attention it needed. And that made Mom crazy, or at least gave her a good excuse to have some hysterical meltdown every time she got nervous about her high-society plans: drop cloths in the living room when company was on the way, when she was hosting another ridiculous benefit or kissing up to historical-society ladies. Our mom's parents would invariably shell out whatever was necessary to make the place exactly what she wanted, but Dad always insisted on doing the work himself—he'd been a carpenter since he was a kid. Even with our nice house Dad's family was a little too close to the wind-beaten lobster-trawling trash our mother liked to pretend didn't exist. Dad always had sawdust in his hair.

But next door it was a very different story. You could tell once the moving van wasn't blocking the black Mercedes and the red Audi that were parked in the driveway that the people who moved in wouldn't be getting much plaster and paint in their hair. I caught all these details right away. Ally of course was out by the wooded edge of our property pick-ing blueberries like she did every Saturday and humming to herself, not having the slightest idea what was going on next door.

She walked over and gave me a handful of blueberries and we stood near the wide-trunked pine in our front yard munching them together. Then a boy came out of the garage and walked between the two fancy cars. We watched him.

He was thin and his shoulders were broad and his hands were covered with engine grease. His hair was an unruly blond mess, his bangs brushed over to the side, and he looked like he'd just woken from a long nap. He had big blue eyes that looked like they were just beginning to focus, like a baby's eyes, like some kind of dazed animal. He had a wrench in the back pocket of his jeans and you could see his ribs through his shirt.

"Nice hairdo!" I called out to him. He flinched as I said it and started walking quickly to his house, flattening his hair down with his dirty hands. But then Ally called out again. Of course she did—the good girl, the sensitive girl that she was.

"Want some blueberries?" she asked him in that way she had, that sweet way like nothing is ever really wrong. "I just picked them. They're special welcome-to-the-neighborhood berries."

She crossed our driveway and handed him the basket. And I watched him standing there, looking at her, then looking down, awkwardly eating blueberries with his dirty hands. Then he smiled. I remember his teeth were unnaturally straight and white and his face was smooth like he didn't need to shave yet—or like he was one of those guys who might never really need to shave. An angelic face but something else behind his eyes.

"What grade are you in?" she asked him.

I could barely make out what he said because he spoke so quietly.

"I'm taking some time off," he said, and then cleared his throat as if he weren't used to talking much. "Ah. I just got here."

She should have walked back into our yard right then and gone inside. But she stood chatting like she always did. The professional hostess's daughter. The golden-haired good girl, unable to see what damage looks like, even when it's staring her right in the face.

* * *

That was then. This is now. If you can call this period of time anything at all. It feels like simply waiting. I guess all that exists is the present. We know what the past got us, and the future . . . well, the future is unwritten. All I know is that I'm almost out of time. I've got less than twelve hours to save myself and to make sure no one, absolutely no one, has to go through what Ally went through. I'm hoping she told me everything she knew, but given the things I found out—the things I know she didn't or couldn't tell me—that seems unlikely. If I could only get the details straight. If only there wasn't something ominous and terrifying floating just below the water's surface out by the slips.

But if I'm going to wish, if I'm going to say "if only," I would go back much further than that. I'd go back to when Ally and me were just kids and I'd fix things before they got bad.

ALLYSON

When I go over it in my head I always start with the morning we met Graham.

I was up early helping Mom get the house ready because the ladies from Rockland Historical Society were coming to look at our widow's walk. Dad had restored it just the way it was in the town's records from the 1920s and now you could go and stand up there and see the whole harbor; you could actually see some of the boats Dad built out in the slips, tall and majestic, and rocking easily on the cold waves. It was beautiful.

I baked some muffins and made some lemon curd and then helped clear up some of Dad's junk. One of the ladies visiting that morning was my boss, Ginny Porter, who owned the Pine Grove Inn. I still couldn't believe I got to have a job in that old mansion. There was a glorious view from nearly every window. On one side you could see the close majesty of tall pines, on the other there were cliffs and the rocky shoreline and the lovely old lonely lighthouse standing tall in the harbor. Because of that job I also got to meet interesting people coming to our town from all over the world. People passing through for a night, or staying for a few days to take it all in. People trying to get away from the city and just relax.

Mom was mortified thinking that our guests would show up early that morning and Daddy would still have his blueprints and models spread all over the dining room, but I was more worried about Sydney, who could be unpredictable when we had company. Either she would say something rude or sulk around in her black skinny jeans and uncombed hair looking like someone owed her something. And if people talked to her God only knew what she'd say. It could be brilliant—like really brilliant, reciting some poem or doing some cool card trick Dad taught us when we were kids—or it could be just plain vicious, calling people snobs or philistines. She loved the word *philistine*. I'd had to look it up. I never heard anyone but her and maybe my social studies teacher use it. This was the thing with Syd: she seemed all dark and tough and low-class if you didn't know her, but she spent so much time with her face in a book she had this vocabulary that shocked people. Since we were little she was like this. Anyway, the word means someone who is hostile to culture. Which I think is completely the opposite of Mom's friends. They all care so much about culture and about the town's history and about genealogy. But whatever. It's not like Syd and I ever really saw things the same way.

Sydney was lying around our room in her black tank top reading (of course) and listening to Bright Eyes or Death Cab or some other weird emo band that sounded like they were whining all alone from the bottom of the ocean. Not exactly the right music for ladies deciding if our house will be designated a historic landmark.

I walked in and handed her a muffin on this cute patterned china plate that we used to have tea parties with, and she sat up, her black tangled mane falling around her shoulders. She had her lost-in-another-world look and she was reading a book that sure wasn't part of the summer reading list for school. *Winter's Bone* I think it was, some creepy thing where everyone's poor and everyone dies. Her side of the room was plastered with posters of the same emo bands plus Brody Dalle from the Distillers, all tattooed and screaming, and a big poster of Tony Hawk upside down above a flight of concrete stairs holding his skateboard, looking like he was about to come crashing down right on Sydney's bed. Which I'm sure she would have just loved.

"Hey, cutie, can you turn it down a little?" I asked.

"Why?" She yawned. "Those blue-haired mummies won't be here for hours."

"Mommy's trying to concentrate on her presentation."

"You're seventeen, Ally. You really should stop calling Liz *Mommy*."

"And you should *not* call Mom Liz," I told her. "It's disrespectful."

"Whatever." She shut her book and took a bite of the muffin and smiled in spite of herself.

I sat down on the bed and thought I could smell cigarette smoke on her clothes, or worse, pot. Great, I thought, just great. I needed to get her out of the house for a while so she wouldn't embarrass Mom or say something weird to Ginny.

"C'mon, smarty," I said, poking her in the sides a little to make her jump. "Let's go pick some berries."

She groaned and made a big show of getting up and putting on her shorts.

Syd can be really difficult sometimes but I've found that if you get her used to an idea there will be less fighting later on. I hated fighting with her. Honestly, I love her too much and don't really have the heart for it. Unlike Syd I've never really been much of a fighter. I remember seeing her when Mom brought her back from the hospital. Her hands already balled into tiny fists. But her birth was a blessing in so many ways. The year she was born was the year I learned how to say no. And that's an important skill for a girl to have.

I dragged her out of the room that morning and we went down the back stairs and rummaged in the pantry for baskets and then headed for the wooded edge of our property. Movers were coming and going from the house next door and Syd wanted to spy and see who our new neighbors would be. I left her by the big old pine and went to pick berries by myself. At least she was out of the house.

The next thing I knew she was shouting. I looked up and saw a tall, sweet-looking kid walking out of the garage across the driveway, cleaning his hands on a rag and carrying a neat little tool kit. He was handsome, his neat blond hair parted on the side and swept across his forehead. He had broad shoulders and you could see his muscles and ribs beneath his shirt. He had that same faraway look Syd gets when she's reading.

"Hey, loser," Sydney called to him. "Nice haircut. You know most Justin Bieber wannabes are twelve years old, right?"

I could see she'd hurt his feelings, that he was a sensitive boy. He started heading for his house, cleaning what must have been the rest of the engine grease off his hands as he walked between the two fancy cars that were parked in his driveway.

"Wait," I called. "Wanna come over here and eat some blueberries? We just picked them."

He stopped and smiled tentatively, tucked the rag into the back pocket of his jeans, and came into our front yard. He smelled clean, like citrus and laundry detergent, and the air around him was cool, as if he had just come out of an air-conditioned room.

Sydney stood close to him, her arms folded across her

chest, sizing him up. The sun shone between the needles of our giant pine, creating a beautiful pattern of light across the ground, dappling their faces with sunshine.

"I'm Tate," she said, in her tough, abrupt way.

He looked at us and then laughed shyly. "I'm Graham," he told us.

"What books do you read?" she asked him, her chin pointed up defiantly. Just like that. Like it's all she cared about. And if you weren't one of her friends—Declan or Becky or some other weird angry brainiac—this could really put you off.

He tossed a handful of blueberries into his mouth and seemed to think about it for a while, too timid to talk. I could tell he was cautious for a reason but I didn't know what that reason might be.

"Anything about art or movies. Anything cars or driving," he said finally. "Or ancient cultures . . ." He looked like he was thinking of more subjects and she smiled faintly at him, gave just the tiniest nod of approval.

Apparently, he wasn't put off at all. It turned out to be the right question. These two will have something to talk about, I thought. I like school but I'm not so interested in heavy reading. I could tell right away he was like Syd. She was the smartest girl in her grade. And the absolute worst for discipline. It was embarrassing for me because they were always calling her down to the office on the PA. I mean rarely a day would go by when there wasn't some trouble

Ms. Tate was getting into. Maybe this kid was going to be a good influence on her, be her friend, I thought as I went back inside and left them talking. I was happy that Sydney was out of the house and out of Mom's hair and that the shy boy seemed to be okay.

But I know now that this was a mistake. I know that thinking things were fine was the biggest mistake I ever made. It's hard for me to talk about all this now after what happened. I feel guilty even remembering. Thinking about how I didn't listen to her. How I ignored everything she said. I guess I was like everyone else, her teachers and her little group of friends at the skate park, Declan and Becky. Everyone thought she was so strong and so smart that she didn't need anything or anyone. People blamed Graham but they should have blamed me. I should have loved her better. Nothing should have come between us.

Especially not a boy.

GRAHAM

4:15—Outside of school playground
7:56—Euclid Avenue parking lot
19:32—Beachfront, slips
23:20—From roof of shed

Dear Lined Piece of Paper,

If I didn't have this journal I wouldn't really talk to anyone, so I guess a lined piece of paper is better than nothing. Dr. Adams says anything is better than nothing, but he has yet to convince me. I'll do my own reading on these subjects.

Okay. Where do I start? They gave my camera back. Obviously. That was a hard one. For a while I thought I might never see it again. But Kim insisted. Because Kim is cool. She gets it. I don't even know where the hell me and Dad would be if he hadn't married her. I certainly never would have been able to keep the camera. And once I get the car fixed up I'll be able to drive it again. I miss driving the most, I guess—just being able to take off and be free and go nowhere.

They say what doesn't kill you makes you stronger. But this was not what I was thinking back before Rockland, when I tried to see if I could in fact break out of this world and into some dark, cool calm that would let me be happy all the time. I was not going for the "make you stronger" part. I was not going for the "what doesn't kill you" part. I was going for peaceful silence. To be able to capture that moment between strength and destruction once and for all. I guess I miscalculated a little.

But that doesn't mean I'll give up. I can try again. I'm making art, like Kim says. And maybe I can make an even better movie than the one me and Eric made back in Virginia. I'm going to stay dedicated to it no matter how many stupid doctors I have to talk to or new pills I have to try. I am going to get around all these people—the ones who always keep trying to convince you to be a part of their dull world, telling you how important you are and how much you mean to them and how you should get up and go for a walk or go to classes and meet new people, or—the stupidest one ever—"do something that will make you happy."

And the constant suggestion that I should "try to focus." Like I can't focus. I pay more attention than anyone I know—twice the amount of attention, especially if I have my camera with me. Then I'm thinking about how everything is going to look. And when I watch it later I don't miss a thing. I think that's the mistake people make—thinking that I'm missing something. I see this world clear as day. I see how everyone plays their part, says what they think other people want to hear. And I see how there are spaces where people are themselves. And that's where I want to go. I want to see them there. Not in school, not trying to be good around their parents or trying to be an example for their kids or trying to look important at work. There is a time when people are entirely themselves, and that's what I want to film. That's the world I want to live in.

What would make me happy is finding another friend like Eric. Eric and I were happy making movies and cruising in the Austin Healey. "Becoming immortal," he called it sometimes when we were driving fast, shooting the passing countryside. Becoming stars. But like stars in the universe—remote and bright and cold and shining. Real stars.

Nobody was going to make me pay for what I did, but instead of being happy about it, all I could think about was getting it right this time. You know what? Maybe I am stronger now. Maybe I should just say fuck it. Because if I'm honest I don't know if I even feel like I need to pay for anything at all. Maybe I did for a minute, maybe I do sometimes when I talk to Dr. Adams—not pay I guess but "process," like he says, and "understand." But this is what I understand: life's not fair. And if I'm doing the things that "make me happy" they might be different from what makes everyone else happy.

I lied earlier about having no one to talk to. I met someone today. And she smiled at me in this way that made me feel like she knew me. Like she knew exactly who I was. I would love to be around someone who knew exactly who I was just for even a minute. It would be such a relief. We talked for about half an hour, standing in the driveway, and I could tell she really gets things.

I was almost going to ask her if she wanted to come into the garage and see the Austin Healey.

It's so close to being fixed.

I do have to give Dad credit for that. Making me fix it myself. And then showing me how. He even had it brought from Virginia so I could keep working on the engine now that I've got the body smoothed out and painted.

I thought after the accident that he would freak, that he'd sell it for parts and never let me drive again. My first thought when I saw how much damage it took was that there was no way it'd ever run again, and that was a real disappointment. My first thought was that it was another miscalculation. Another thing Eric and I didn't see coming. Sometimes I wish we could talk about it. It would really help if I could just ask him a few questions. My second thought was that maybe I was made of steel. Maybe I was unbreakable. I could watch the rest of the world slip away—I could record it—but I was here to stay.

"It's a lesson," Dad said.

And Kim, my stepmom, said, "It's an opportunity."

Either way the Austin Healey is almost ready to get back on the road, and I'm almost ready to start school again. I'm not sure how I feel about going to this school. But maybe it will be different.

The only thing I miss about Virginia is Eric. I wish I could hang out with him again. Though I can't say I'm completely sorry about the way things turned out. Eric made me understand who I am. Eric made me know what the world is really like and what I am capable of. And if it weren't for all the stupid bullshit from his parents, Eric would already be famous.

Maybe I'll talk to that Tate girl at school. Maybe I can see her alone. I felt when I went back into the new house like I wanted to see her again right away, like I needed to. I went up to my room and looked next door and wondered which window was hers. About an hour later I headed back to the garage and I thought I saw her standing in the big square cupola on top of their house, looking out over the harbor, over the tops of the giant pines.

She was like Helen of Troy, standing up there in the glass room beneath the blue sky with the clouds rolling in from the ocean. I wanted to be able to look at her always. Wanted a film of her just standing there. I could film her doing anything and it would be interesting. Just talking. Just saying nothing.

I could suddenly see how wars could be fought over beauty. And I wanted to film her for the rest of her life.

SYDNEY

My locker was nearly side by side with Allyson's on the second floor by the stairs, which meant she could easily leave yellow sticky notes on it reminding me about chores we had at home or just offering her usual sisterly good cheer. Like: "Hi, Cutie!" or just a picture of a talking cat with a bow on its head—I guess that was supposed to be Hello Kitty. She dotted her i's with hearts and every time I saw one of these sparkly, bubble-written monstrosities I nearly barfed. Imagine having to listen to the *Barney* theme song on permanent repeat. That's what it was like getting these notes. There was nothing wrong with them—they all said nice things—but somehow everything about them was wrong.

"Oh my God," Becky said, pulling the latest one down, sticking it to the front of my sweater, and reading it. "Do you really have to meet your mom downtown at the historical society after school? I was hoping we could take the back way home and get in a little four-twenty action on the way."

Becky was wearing her headphones, a red-and-gray flannel shirt, and black skinny jeans. She fiddled distractedly with her new nose ring, a small silver hoop that looked like it might already be irritating an infection. She had a wide mouth and full lips and small square teeth. And she polished her nails so that every other finger had black or red nail polish on it. Today she was wearing a gauzy scarf with little skulls all over it. Lockers were slamming shut all around us and voices were raised and slightly rowdy at the end of the day, just kids happy to be getting out, happy to have a couple hours of freedom before it started all over again.

Of course I wasn't going to meet my mom downtown. Becky didn't even need to ask. Mom wanted to get Ally and me some new shoes. She could get them for Ally. I'd just broken in my slip-on Vans and I had no intention of seeing what her idea of a fashionable pair of shoes looked like. I had a closet full of things my mom thought were so "me." This is "so you!" she would say, holding up a pair of low pink wedges. Or: "This would look *great* on you!" holding a powder-blue silk blouse up just below my chin and taking a step back to nod approvingly. "Stunning."

Ally loved this kind of thing, and she generally *did* look stunning in whatever Mom picked out for her. But these shopping outings weren't my thing. I always felt like I was being dressed like a poodle. It was an outfit or shoes for my mother, not for me. It was an outfit or shoes that would make my mother look good because she had a daughter who had fancy clothes or looked pretty. Sometimes when I was out with her I felt like a bracelet she owned and not her daughter. And I always heard it when Ally was standing beside her: "She's so pretty!" they'd say—right in front of Ally as if she didn't exist at all. As if she was something my mother had bought for herself.

I pulled the yellow sticky note off my shirt and crumpled it into a ball, dropping it into the bottom of the locker where it landed on a pile of maybe two hundred other crumpled yellow notes.

"Yeah, four twenty sounds good to me," I said.

"Hell yeah," Becky said, and laughed.

I put my history and science books away and jammed that evening's homework into my backpack, turning around just in time to see Declan Wells striding up the stairs two at a time, his bag over one shoulder, his board under his arm, and his wavy black hair falling around his shoulders.

"Speak of the devil," I whispered to Becky. Though it was hardly by chance that he appeared. Declan met us upstairs at our lockers every day after school.

He stopped in front of us and bent his head to the side. "Aw, yeah. Does someone need a little mental vacation from the strain and stress of pretending all goddamn day that we are not really living in some tedious made-for-TV movie about the failure of the education system, the folly of youth, and the burgeoning surveillance culture? A little lift perhaps? A little journey to a softer world?"

Becky and I looked at each other, shook our heads, and grinned. Declan could never just say "Hey, homies." Or "What's up?" He loved to hear himself speak too much—but then again we loved to hear him too. That boy always made me smile.

I pulled my skateboard out of my locker and set it on the smooth gray tiled floor, then stood on it to make myself as tall as Declan, folding my arms across my chest. I looked right into his wide-set dark-brown eyes and then he laughed, almost to himself. "Yes? Ms. Tate? You have something to share with us?"

"I'm up!" I said, then pushed off and maneuvered down the hall on my board against the steady stream of kids headed out for the day. I turned and glanced back to make sure he was looking, then did a perfect, tight kick flip right in front of the upstairs office.

"She's crazy," I heard him say in that admiring tone—the one he had where he sounded excited, like he might almost laugh. I looked back just in time to see Becky nod in agreement and then watched as they both stopped short. Mr. Fitzgerald leaned out of his office and called my name.

"Tate! How many times have I told you not to skate in the hall?"

"Probably thirty," I called back to him. "Maybe forty. But who's counting?"

Declan and Becky stifled their laughter.

"Carry that board *out* of the building or I *will* confiscate it this time."

I flipped the skateboard up into my hands and kept walking, ignoring him. Becky and Declan followed behind me.

"'Sup, Mr. Fitz?" Declan said as they passed. "Happy to go home after a long day as guardian of America's future rocket scientists and Walmart greeters?"

Fitz said, "Watch yourself, Wells. Have a good afternoon, Becky. Oh, just a minute . . . Wells, we have a new student starting next week. He'll need to shadow someone for a day and get shown the ropes, and guess who's going to be doing the showing?"

"Aw, serious? Me? I'm not like Virgil or something, you know, guiding some newbie through hell. That's really not the archetype I prefer, Mr. Fitz."

Mr. Fitzgerald smiled and shook his head. "Nice Dante reference, Wells. You have such a good brain in there. Maybe your attitude could catch up to it, huh? And guess what? You *are* gonna be Virgil for a day or some of those missed detentions are going to magically multiply. The student's name is Graham Copeland. Nice kid. Getting a little bit of a late start and I think he needs someone like you to show him around."

"C'mon!" I yelled from the end of the hallway. I didn't hear everything Fitz had said but I'm sure it wasn't worth spending another two seconds of our lives at school. "Half pipe's awaiting! And so's the other pipe."

They caught up to me and we ran downstairs and out into the parking lot. Becky was already taking the little bowl out of the top pocket of her flannel and she started packing it as we walked. She could barely get through the day anymore without medicinal help. She'd just started getting high a couple months ago but she was already making up for lost time. Usually she would smoke right after school, then go straight to her room and listen to LCD Soundsystem's *Sound of Silver* over and over again while she wrote computer code and did other hacker things that were so geeky even me and Declan could barely understand her. She also made jewelry out of sea glass and superglue and wire that she gave to people as gifts. It was like some kind of stoned Santa's workshop in her room with electronic music instead of Christmas carols.

And she was running out of people to give them to. Their cleaning lady already had two necklaces, a bracelet, and three sets of earrings. And the cleaning lady's kid had a sea glass necklace she had made him that he'd drawn a big *W* on with a Sharpie marker. "For Wolverine," he told her. I had a whole cigar box full of necklaces. Some of which I'd just hang in the windows of my room to catch the light. Declan took her sea glass stuff and actually put it back in the sea. "It'll get better with time," he told her when she caught him doing it. Before Becky started getting high, she used to do schoolwork with the same intense concentration. But now it was just coding and sea glass and she seemed much happier now.

"What did Fitz want?" Becky asked, brushing her long red hair out of her face as we ducked beneath the low branches that hung before the footpath down to the creek. The fall leaves crunched beneath our feet and the air smelled good, like autumn: wood smoke and mud and pine and the faint brackish salty smell of the ocean that hung in the air all around.

Declan said, "He wanted me to show some new kid around. I swear, he thinks just 'cause of my PSAT scores, I always gotta represent the school or some bullshit."

"It's your own fault," I said. "You could stop winning chess games and science fairs and maybe drop out of the Model UN and debate team. The reason he got that idea is because you actually *do* represent the school. Duh."

Becky nodded in agreement. "Shoulda done the wake-and-bake method of studying for the P-sat," she said, inhaling deeply and passing the bowl to him. She coughed and smiled. "I think that helped knock me down to average from slightly above. Except in math."

I rolled my eyes. "I don't think anything could depose you from being the scary computer math nerd queen," I said. "Anyway, who's the kid?"

"Graham somebody."

I couldn't believe my ears. "Graham Copeland?!" I shouted. "Gross. That's the creepy fucking dweeb I was telling you about."

I took the bowl from Declan. Becky was laughing at the way I'd said "creepy dweeb," or maybe the way a squirrel had run across our path, or she was just laughing because, as usual, she was high or thinking about something else when other people were talking—I couldn't tell which.

Declan shrugged. "The car kid?"

"Creepy dweeb," Becky said to herself, snickering.

"Oh my God, you'll be with him all day and telling him about school? This is too good. You have to tell me all about him." I handed Becky the bowl and grinned back at Declan. "I just know there's something weird going on there. There's a story in there that we don't know."

Declan shrugged. "Your motivations seem suspect, Tate. Him being a dweeb or a nerd or socially outside the norm is hardly a reason for me to spy on him, but perhaps you'd like to simply admit to us how you feel about this creeb. This dewy breec, this weepy bed wrec."

"Oh God! Stop with the anagrams!" Becky yelled. "He's worse with the anagrams when he's stoned," she told me, but of course I already knew this.

"It's true," I said, looking at Declan. I don't think those even count as anagrams. Weepy Bed Wreck? He's just making up words.

"I'm simply saying that if you want me to *spy* on him because *you* feel hormonally compelled to spend time with him, you might as well just say so."

Becky looked at me, rolled her eyes, then started laughing

again. Declan grabbed me around the waist and spun me in a circle. "Tate's got a crush!" he said, and then kissed me.

"You know who I've got a crush on," I told him, looking right into his eyes.

He smiled at me, returned the look. "Life's long, Tate. There's lots of crushes to have."

The woods were becoming prettier by the second and I was happy to be there with my two best friends. We walked along the trail out to where it met back up with the road that led to our neighborhood. Then I put the skateboard back down on the pavement.

"Of course I'll check him out for you," Declan said.

"Can we please go buy some Doritos now?" Becky asked. "Or cake. Oh! You know what would be good? Cupcakes. My mom made some yesterday. Let's go to my place."

"I'm gonna skate," I told them. The fact was I loved skating when I was a little high. There was a good winding downhill to my house and almost never any cars and it felt amazing to cruise down it right to the door of my house. "See you tomorrow."

"Bye!" they yelled in unison, grinning and looking like the coolest people you could ever spend an afternoon with. I watched them turn around and walk beneath the trees that flanked the sides of the road, leaves just beginning to turn yellow and hope and mystery filling our whole small world. Then I got on my board and leaned into the curve, coasting home.

To: harlanadams@mind2mindpsychotherapy.com
From: david.copeland@copelandconsulting.com

Dear Dr. Adams,

We'd like to thank you for all the help you've given Graham over the last year.

As you know, he will be starting school again next week, and we are beginning to feel some trepidation. Kim has mentioned again the possibility of homeschooling—she would be able to stay home with him and has the credentials to teach him, and we feel they have as strong a relationship as a boy like Graham could have with a stepparent. We were wondering if you could advise us. I'm sure you understand our concerns, and I'm wondering if maybe this is the best route to take.

I know you've said it's important for him to get some socialization, and while we essentially agree, the fear and risk of reliving anything close to what happened in Virginia has made us very reticent. We're concerned that his social life be a healthy one. We don't want to see any more heartache.

We've read the books you recommended about the benefits of combining drug regimens with talk therapy, and in theory we are fully ready to support Graham any way we can, but in practice it seems daunting.

He's still working on the Austin, and I'm planning on

buying him another antique car for Christmas, which I think will also be therapeutic. And we're getting him that better telescope he wanted. Trying to encourage his healthy preoccupations. His mechanical skills are really quite excellent, and the best times we have together are in the garage just tinkering. Or outside looking at the stars.

We've tried harder than anyone to put the past behind us and invested as much as a family can in the health of our child. We've come a long way from last year. But I would be lying if I said that I wasn't still afraid of my own son sometimes. I'm hoping that you can give us the best advice. We agree that his spending should be monitored, and there's no need for him to have his own source of income at this point. He's getting his usual allowance, and we make purchases for him. I'm happy to update you regularly as we make this transition.

Also we know that there have been some advancements in the drug regimens since Graham was prescribed, and we'd like to make sure he's on the best possible plan. Please let us know about any pharmaceuticals you think could make this time easier for him. Thank you again for your support.

Best,

David Copeland

SYD

After that first day when we saw him out by his car, it seemed like he was always around. I would almost say *lurking* around but it was his own house, so I guess you'd just call it hanging out. Most of the time he was working on his fancy car or filming things.

Once when I was practicing some tricks in the driveway he came over and asked if he could film me—you know, doing kick flips and simple stuff.

I shrugged. "Sure," I said. "Do you skate?" He had the tall, lanky, hair-in-your-eyes look that kinda said *skater*, so it was a reasonable question.

"Nah," he said. "I'm afraid I'll break my neck."

I laughed and then skated over to him, stepped off the board. "Here," I said. "Give it a try. You'll be fine."

He smiled nervously and put his foot on the board. And when I looked up into his face, his eyes looked really funny.

Like his pupils were huge. Big black disks in the center of blue. Whoa, I thought, maybe he *will* break his neck if he's going to try skating all messed up on whatever he's messed up on. He stepped onto the board and just stood there and that's when I noticed Ally walking down the driveway carrying a wicker lunch basket.

"My sister can do some good driveway tricks too," I said.

He raised his eyebrows. "Oh yeah?"

"Yeah, you should ask her about it sometime."

Ally sat on the low wall near the house and just watched us. She gave me a funny, skeptical look—the kind that said, "That boy can't skate," and I almost laughed out loud.

Sometimes she could get that kind of look our father had where he would just stare blankly and then ask what kind of boats you'd sailed. Graham didn't look like he could keep himself upright on a skateboard, so I doubted he had any sea legs. And things like sea legs were pretty important to Ally, who still sailed with our dad quite a bit.

"So, um. How do I do it?" Graham asked.

"Skate!" I said.

He looked a little confused and then put his foot on the board and pushed along the pavement. The driveway sloped down and curved into the woods. By the time he had reached the end of the slope he had fallen off. He lay there on his back dramatically while I trudged down the driveway. Then I stood over him with my hands on my hips. He was gazing up into the sky with a weird look on his face, a half smile, his eyes drifting from left to right as they followed a cloud.

I looked back at Ally, who was grinning and shaking her head. Then she headed back toward the woods with her basket to pick berries.

I said "All right, captain head case, point taken. You cannot skate. Hand over the board."

I shrugged and hopped back on the board and skated around his body, then up the driveway and retrieved his camera from where he left it, handed it to him. But I get you, I thought. Behind those dilated eyes is a great big secret.

ALLY

I rode my blue vintage Schwinn along the winding coastal road to work, feeling the wind blowing my hair around my shoulders. My baby-blue helmet was buckled beneath my chin and I had on my powder-blue silk shirt Mom had bought me and my jean jacket, and my backpack was full of homework. Always so much homework. Sometimes I wished I could be like Sydney and never have to study. It's not like I couldn't get good grades, but I had to concentrate and work twice as hard as she did. I knew working hard was one of the best qualities a person could have, but I still felt dumb sometimes. It's not easy to have a little sister who is so brainy.

I thought about college applications while I rode. I hoped admissions at Emerson would appreciate how hard I'd been working, hoped it reflected in the transcripts I'd be sending. I knew that my recommendations would be good but worried about my grades in English and science, worried that my essay might be a little boring. I started working on it over the summer even though it wasn't due for several months. I'd even shown it to Sydney—who had actually had some good suggestions and helped a lot. Guess Syd couldn't wait for me to get out of the house, wanted to make sure she got me into school and away.

I think Syd and I were like two sides of the same coin. She wouldn't work at anything that didn't interest her but she had some kind of crazy memory for information. I would work at everything as hard as I could but things slipped my mind all the time. It was hard to keep hold of facts. I liked practical things better and I felt like there was always enough going on to keep me busy. I was like that since we were little. I often felt like Sydney did things and I just watched her do them and made sure she didn't get hurt. For example she'd never wear a helmet if she was riding a bike. She almost never wore one when she was skating.

That might seem brave, but another word for it is reckless—or maybe even stupid. I liked to have fun too, but I didn't think the fun came from the possibility that you might get hurt. If Daddy said to put on a life jacket when we were on the boat and it was stormy, I put on a life jacket. I wore a helmet when I rode my bike. Syd thought things like that made me scared or wimpy, but I enjoyed what I did.

I loved biking away on the hills or along the ocean and being alone and away from everyone, feeling free and smelling the salt air and thinking about nothing. I really did think about nothing. I'm not embarrassed to say it. It was a gift. Most people can't stop thinking about who they are or what they'll do or what people think about them but I could. I could stop thinking about upsetting things and think about nothing. I could accept the world just as it is and live in it just fine. When life gives you blueberries, bake blueberry muffins!

I always thought one day, maybe when we're older we'd become better friends and see how what we thought were opposite qualities actually complemented each other. Just like Mom's and Dad's.

The leaves were just beginning to change color and the stunning yellows and flame reds whizzed past and crunched beneath my tires in the gutter. The breeze smelled like wood smoke and crisp fall air and it was still warm where it was sunny. I loved days like that. The bright hot sun and the high round clouds made me feel free, like I could do anything.

When I arrived at Pine Grove, I locked my bike out front and then went in to say hi to Ginny. I would be changing linens for the first hour and then would relieve the other receptionist at the front desk. Maybe if there were few calls or little to do I'd get to do some schoolwork before biking back home. The place always smelled like vanilla candles and cinnamon, and the old wood was polished shiny and clean, and the wide plank floors creaked a little beneath the traditional braided rugs Ginny had bought down at the antiques market. The whole place was cozy and charming, like stepping into the past.

The sofa in the lobby was also an antique and Ginny had made a log cabin quilt to throw over the arm. It all looked so perfect and made me happy we live in New England. I honestly couldn't think of anywhere else I'd like to live. Rockland suited me fine and I was proud my family had lived there for generations; it seemed to make the memories all sweeter and deeper, all of us decades after decades going to the same schools, walking down the same roads.

I looked out the windows at the beautiful ocean. It was always so quiet and peaceful there. I was lucky to get paid to sit in that pretty room. Work was usually fun and laid-back. A few guests checking in, a phone reservation or two. But that evening, there must have been something wrong with the telephone connections at the front desk, or maybe a wireless tower had gone down nearby.

Because a few times every hour I would get a call and no one would be on the other line.

I would answer. I would say, "Hello, hello?" And there would be nothing but silence and then a cold quiet click.

POLICE CHIEF BILL WERTZ

responded to the call in the late afternoon. Shocked to hear it on the scanner. And I fully expected it to be some contractor who'd had too much to drink at Kelley's Dockside Happy Hour. But it wasn't. There was already a small crowd there. It was a chilly day, but bright, and the sun was just beginning to get low in the sky—reflecting out across the water. You never would have known on a day so normal and beautiful that something could go so horribly wrong. People never expect it, but in my experience, that's when it happens.

I patrolled the harbor regularly and I'd been used to breaking up some or other nonsense, carpenters who had maybe a few too many, kids who were bothering the yacht owners with their music or smoking or skateboarding. But mostly I would be cruising by and making sure things were as they should be. And in Rockland, hell, in Rockland things usually were. People kept to themselves for the most part. Yeah, maybe the rich folks stay up in their neighborhoods or at the yacht club or country club or the golf course. Maybe us regular folks go down to the seaside public parks to grill and play baseball. Make picnics and let the kids play at the shore. What I'm saying is the town didn't mingle a lot. There was a big old divide between the west and east side, but folks didn't mean each other any harm. Not here.

I don't know how to say this without just saying it. When strangers move to town, things get shaken up. People from away don't quite fit in—not down at the park and not up at the golf course either. And you gotta wonder why they left where they were from in the first place. I knew it when I was in the ambulance staring down at that kid. This isn't the kind of problem we have here, I thought to myself. This just isn't the kind of thing we do. And I shoulda known. I shoulda known all along. I shoulda never dropped my guard, been charmed, been taken in. The fact was I saw it coming, I'd been warned. I might be just a small-town cop but I've been around the block and I knew the kinds of things that go on in this world.

I'd dragged bodies out of the water before—this is Maine and it gets cold and the water gets treacherous sometimes. There were tragedies for sure; drowning, boating while intoxicated, a suicide. But this. Nothing like it. I never had to show up at a parent's doorstep and tell them the thing that would destroy their life.

Never. Not until that day.

SYD

I don't know why I wanted Declan to spy on him. I guess I wanted to see what he was really like. At the time I didn't have any information about him, just what I could observe by hanging around. And I have to admit I had a strong reaction whenever I thought of him or when anyone mentioned him. It wasn't even so much that he was handsome—though he certainly was.

Honestly, I just think I was bored. Bored bored bored. Some days I actually feel like I'm trapped in the school. Like the place is really a jail. We're forced by law to go there—to be there all day. It's the closest thing to a prison there is. In fact it's like the whole population actually has to go to prison first before they can enter society. Have to make sure we learn these arbitrary bullshit rules—make sure we won't talk back, that we'll follow orders. Once we prove that, once they've ruined our ability to even think for ourselves—then they let us go.

Declan was right about having to pretend we're not in some tedious made-for-TV movie. It's not like you really have to study. If you pay attention for even one minute you know what's going on. I used to beg my parents to let me stay home and read something good instead of wasting my time at school, but then Ally liked school so much I'd just get dragged along with her—sucked into her idea about it. That didn't last forever obviously but when I was young she'd always coax me to get up in the morning and tell me how much fun class was going to be.

After a while it was anything but fun. I'd be stuck sitting at my desk for hours and hours after I already got it, listening to some teacher who just has a BA from a shitty school and a teaching certificate from the state of Maine drone on and on and on and on instead of being outside skating or reading a good book or listening to music. School might be fine for Ally and her friends but not for me. Not for Declan and Becky either. And I had a feeling—not for Graham. Something about the way he looked at things made me feel like he was already done with whatever it was school was theoretically supposed to offer. Really done. Like he'd already been to college and had a job and two kids and been divorced and remarried and had become an alcoholic and was paying double alimony and child support even though he was just a kid. That's how heavy his look was. He was weary and skittish and somehow weirdly confident; up to something, beaten down but unbeaten. And he was clearly on some kind of drugs. I mean clearly the kid was wasted half the time—or at least that's the impression I got. Sometimes his pupils were dilated and sometimes they were little pinpricks.

"Don't you think you're giving this guy a little too much thought?" Declan very reasonably asked. "I mean, he sounds chill. I'm not really up for spying on some guy because you've got a crush. It doesn't bother *me*; it shouldn't bother *you*. Why don't we just hang with him?"

This was classic Declan. Once he got high he was all philosophical about how "everything in the world is connected" and everyone is chill and we should all get along. And peace and love and God in the smallest drop of water blah blah blah.

"Yeah, a lot of thought," Becky said, and then started laughing. "Too much thought." She looked at us but couldn't keep a straight face. "Is he yummy?" Then she laughed again. "Oh . . . wait . . . no . . . didn't mean to say yummy . . . ," she whispered to herself. "Is he . . . um . . . ?"

"He's like some kind of teen idol," I said, interrupting her weird digression. "It's gross actually. Fancy car, fancy clothes, pretty golden hair, like he belongs in a catalog, except for all the other stuff I told you about. Y'know, how he looks like an old man kinda . . . all serious." I could have gone on and on discussing the details but I got lost thinking about it and then I got distracted looking at the leaves moving gently in the wind.

"Definitely not your type," Declan said, grinning, bringing me back to the conversation. "But he doesn't sound like a creepy dweeb either."

Becky laughed. She said, "Dweepy creeb."

"He is!" I shouted. "Being from a catalog and being a creep are not mutually exclusive. They don't cancel each other out, you can be one and still the other. You can—"

"We get it, we get it," Declan said, waving his hands in front of my face. "It just seems weird of you to be so wrapped up in a guy like that when you only hung out with him *once*. I know you have your Spidey senses, Tate, but maybe they're not working with this dude. I mean, think about who you really want to invest your energy in." He leaned forward, smiled beatifically at me, and batted his eyelashes.

It was funny but I really didn't want Declan to start going on and on about "energy," which was a whole other lecture he liked to give when he was high. "Energy" and then, without fail, physics and string theory and YouTube videos of talking crows. Weed just made Declan more in awe of the world than he already was, which was saying something, and made him talk ten times as much, which could get pretty unbearable—especially if you were also a little effed-up.

I knew what he was getting at by the "my type" comment. Declan was "my type" and he knew it. He was the ranked chess champ of the county, had nearly a perfect score on his PSAT, and he dealt pot and read Dostoyevsky and Jane Austen. That's who I want to be with. That's who I want to run away and sleep on the beach with. That's who I want to give it to and take it from. Not some weird kid from the south. I told myself that again to make sure I really got it. Declan, I thought. Declan, not Graham.

But I had to admit there was some pull I felt from Graham. Like he knew something about me right away. Something other people ignored or just didn't realize. There was a mystery about him that I wanted to understand. The way he laughed when he met me and Ally. The way he looked at Ally. Our fates were twisted. I knew it the minute he crossed into our yard and stood with the sun on his face beneath the pine tree.

I know it seems like even then I was becoming obsessed with him. That I was paying too much attention to him, like Declan said. Now I only wish I had paid more attention. Those cool blue eyes were used to looking at people a certain way. Used to being looked at like he was the black sheep. And he was smart. My only hope, now that time is running out, is that he was never—even at his best— smarter than me.

ALLY

I told Sydney about the calls at work and she made her usual snide comments. She told me that it definitely wasn't some cell tower problem and that probably someone was stalking me and that I should have told Mrs. Porter. It's a little hard to take her ideas seriously sometimes. She can get paranoid and see the worst in everything. I told her I'd tell Ginny Porter if it happened again but that I wasn't going to jump to any conclusions about anything or take advice from someone dressed head to toe in black. "Can you get out the sugar?" I asked her. I was reading a new scone recipe.

"You're ignoring me!" she shouted.

"I think I'll put walnuts in these," I told her, and she groaned and slapped her forehead dramatically.

"Listen to me, Ally," she said. "Has anything like that ever happened at work before?"

"Not that I remember," I said, cutting the butter into small squares and pouring a cup of sugar into the bowl.

Syd was overreacting as usual and I think this time it was because she was jealous. The fact is Syd can be jealous of my job. It's probably the only thing she *is* jealous of. I don't think there's anything else she pays attention to. She's jealous of my job because she's unemployable. She interviewed for positions at other B and Bs in town and did not get them. Too busy hanging out skating with Becky and Declan to really make an effort to get dressed up and submit a résumé and look like she was interested in the places. And I think people could tell by looking at her that she was a little wild.

She said, "Whatever, Ally. Suit yourself. I'm going over to Declan's!" That was her solution to everything. She barely spent any time at home anymore. And if you said something that made her upset or contradicted her, she went over to Declan's.

I like Becky and Declan fine. Even though they act like I don't exist. I remember the first time Declan came over and Syd brought him to our room. He looked at her posters and he looked at mine—looked at the stuff on my side of the room—and he laughed really hard. Right in front of me. He said, "You're a master of irony." I walked out of the room. I'm sure they needed their privacy anyway.

Becky, I actually like a lot. I mean she and Syd have been friends since they were little kids. And we used to play together sometimes. My friends, of course, don't want to spend time around Syd at all. So I stopped introducing her to them. I generally see them at school or at work. The few times I tried to hang out with her and one of my friends she was really rude. We were baking a quiche together and she wouldn't help with anything or clean up. She just sat on the counter, swinging her feet, acting bored, and kinda making fun of us. She kept saying, "So who's your boyfriend?" It was really awkward. Or, "Have you ever even made out with a boy?" Not very classy.

I think the only friend we really had in common was Graham. In fact he may be the only person we really spent time with as sisters—Graham brought us together. At last. But not for very long, obviously. Things went really fast once Graham moved next door. Life changed in the blink of an eye.

SYD

Since Graham moved in it seemed that all he did was mess around with his car. He would keep the garage door open and I had a pretty good view of him from the screened-in porch on the west side of our house. So I would sit out there sometimes and watch him. I didn't feel bad doing this. I knew he watched us too and I knew he was really interested in Allyson.

A lot of the time he would go into the garage with a cup of coffee in his hand, wearing his jeans and a ratty V-neck T-shirt. Sometimes he would stand there looking at the car not doing anything for about half an hour. Other times he'd be bent over the engine.

Something about the way he moved really got to me. I couldn't decide if I liked it or thought he was a creep. His body was more relaxed than Declan's. He seemed lithe like a puppy, but sleepy. He moved slowly. And I could see the muscles in his back when he was leaning over the hood of the car.

Also he was a superrich kid doing manual labor, which seemed like a contradiction somehow. Most of the preppy boys I knew sailed or snowboarded or did other things like that for hobbies. No one rebuilt cars, or fixed things. I liked that he was different, but there was something that seemed dangerous about him. Even by himself—not talking to anyone and tinkering around all alone, he seemed moody. I watched him throw a wrench across the garage because he was frustrated. And another time I watched him sit in the car staring straight ahead—lost in thought, it looked like he was wiping tears out of his eyes.

There was something wrong with Graham. And I wanted to know what it was. I wanted to know what made him the way he was, to be his friend, to talk to him and hang out, to go driving with him. I wanted to know his secrets.

I wanted to make him disappear.

GRAHAM

1:42—Yacht club
5:37—Best Buy
7:00—Woods
18:54—Roof

Dear Lined Piece of Paper,
I have to figure out a way to talk to her. If I had more confidence—just normal confidence—I'd have asked for her digits. I'd have gotten her email at least. I'd have said, "Are you on Facebook?" I would have done whatever regular people do when they meet someone.

What is that anyway? I guess the kind of stuff I used to do with Eric. I'd have taken her for a ride in the Austin, I'd have shown her the screening room in my house or Kim's paintings. And maybe some of the things I didn't do with Eric. But of course I didn't think of any of these things at the time. I thought about

49

kissing her. Right there in the driveway. I thought how nice it would be to just reach out and hold her hand. She was standing so close I don't know how I could have thought of anything else. And I think she must have felt the same way. I'm hoping she did. The way she joked. The way she looked right at me when she talked.

Thanks to Dr. Adams, though, I can fix this shyness. I thought I was taking enough to make me feel a little better in these social situations, but apparently I am not. I mean, I'm fine talking to strangers now and that kind of thing, but being around her made me feel so nervous. The way I used to feel going to school or talking to other kids. So you know what? I'm just going to take more. What can they do about it? Nothing. And besides, I know that taking more makes me feel better. I can't spend my time stammering at the end of a telephone or hanging up or just looking at her out of my window.

I'll never get her to be in my movies if I can't talk to her. Or take her for a ride or go to the beach or anything. I want so badly to just drive. To just drive around with her.

The thing is we all have a choice now about who we want to be. We don't have to be how we were born. If there's a problem, if you don't do something right, you can fix it. That's why these drugs exist in the first place. Imagine what the world was like without them.

SYD

Becky grabbed me after biology class just as I was headed outside to the unofficial smoking lounge—the benches under the big maple just two feet off school property. She had a distant, goofy grin on her face and she was carrying a pile of books.

"Okay. He is actually super freaking HOT!" she said. "Your description did *not* do him justice—he's like actually interesting looking, not just some pretty boy. I don't think there's anything bad about him at all."

"Hello? And you are talking about *who*? A little context here, please . . ."

"Okay. So, this morning I am walking to school and Graham drives by in like this James Bond car or something—but you know, like a James Bond car from the seventies—like Sean Connery James Bond . . . or the one right after him. Who was the one after him?"

I rolled my eyes. "Not *that* much context."

Becky laughed. "And so I just watch him cruise by," she said. "I think, okay, he's cute. But THEN when I got to school I went around back and was sneaking a smoke out by that one corner where they don't have their freaking spy cameras set up and he's STILL sitting in his car.

"C'mon." She pulled me by the arm and started walking back behind the school.

I dragged my feet following her and felt again like this kid had some kind of weird power. My sister, now my best friend—who was next, Declan? Was I the only one who thought there was something weird going on? Was Declan going to be best buds with this kid? But I only had to worry about that one for a second.

"I don't know why you and Declan don't like him," Becky went on, stopping to light her cigarette. "Declan called him a drug addict, which I thought was hilarious. He said his eyes look funny and he seemed too skinny. I was like, YOU? *You* are calling someone a drug addict? You are saying someone is skinny and has red eyes or whatever? YOU, Declan Wells? Okay, whatever."

We rounded the corner of the school and sure enough his car was still parked there. "Oh, sh sh sh," Becky said, as if I had been the one loudly talking about him being a drug addict.

I had rarely seen Becky like this. She could be flighty, but generally she was too cool to get all hung up on some dude. "Oh my God," she whispered. "Look at his car. Is he like the richest person in the world or what? It looks like his clothes are manufactured by magic fairies to fit his body perfectly."

"Jesus, Beck, can you stay focused for like two minutes?"

Graham saw us walking toward the car and waved. We waved back.

"Howdy, neighbor," I said sarcastically when we reached the car. He was sitting there, clearly staring at Becky. Instead of saying hello he just said:

"Can I film you, Becky? I just want some footage of you smoking."

Becky paused like some starstruck twelve-year-old. She exhaled a cloud of smoke into the crisp fall air and laughed shyly.

"Why do you want to film her?" I asked.

"I'm making this movie. It's not a documentary or anything. It's an art film, but it's got real people talking about themselves in it."

"Yeah, sure," Becky said.

And then he took out the tiniest camera I've ever seen and filmed her face really close up, then asked her to say her name and exhale the smoke. He didn't even get out of his car.

"Beautiful," he said. "Perfect." He was completely relaxed and confident in a way I'd never seen him. And Declan was right—his eyes were messed up—not like ours got, bloodshot, but weirder. The pupils were hugely dilated. Sometimes when I saw him they were constricted like little pinpoints but now they were wide, a black void surrounded by a pretty pale-blue ring of iris. But there was no denying he was handsome.

He filmed her for a few more moments. "What's your address?" he asked, and she replied, smiling at him, pushing her hair behind her ears. "Where do you go to school? Do you like it here?" She answered all his questions and then he took a little notebook from the glove compartment and wrote something down.

"So what are you going to do with all this?" Becky asked when he was done.

"I'm going to use it as part of a feature-length movie," he said. "An experimental movie. And hopefully bring it to London with me when I go again with my stepmom. She has some artwork at an auction house there and there's a film festival I want to enter some of my stuff in."

It was interesting, but I don't know if I believed him entirely. I thought he might be lying to impress us, or to get Becky to go out with him.

"Well, thanks, ladies," he said, then put his car in gear. "Bye, Becky." He waved. "See you at home, Tate." Then he drove away. He clearly wasn't planning on going to school that day.

"Uh . . . don't you think that was a little weird?" I asked Becky.

"No, I think it's freaking awesome! He seems like a real

artist. Oh, and I found out he's taking studio art, so I'll see him in there while the rest of you brainiacs are sitting stoned off your ass in Beecher's bullshit chemistry lab. Ha!"

"If he ever shows up," I said.

"Oh, he'll show up, he's FINE. What the hell is it with you? He does all the things you normally like. If I didn't know better I'd say you had a crush on him and you just don't know how to deal. You're acting like a third-grade boy. C'mon, Tate! This is the coolest kid who's moved to town in the history of Rockland and he lives right next DOOR to you. You should be psyched!"

"Maybe," I said. "There's more to people than their cool cars and their pretty clothes."

"Right," said Becky. "There's their cool artwork and cool ideas and awesome bodies. And if he's on drugs, he's on something better than what we've got. We should check that out, no?"

I sighed and shrugged. Maybe I was overreacting. Maybe I did have a crush on him. So little went on in Rockland it was easy to fixate on anything new that came along. And she was right in a way, Graham was cool. It would be something to know how to build a car or make movies. The things we did most were skateboard, talk about how we hated school while actually taking all the best classes and competing for class rank, listening to music and getting high, and wandering around the sleepy harbor town at night.

Graham had had some other, deeper life. It showed on

his skin. I didn't know what it was that drew me to him and made me resist the very idea of hanging out with him at the same time.

Becky tossed her cigarette on the ground and stubbed it out with her toe and then she put her arm around me and we started walking back in to our next classes.

She said, "C'mon, lovebug. I think things are really looking up!"

KIM RAY

My mother told me not to marry an older man who had a child. Too big a restoration project, she said. But I never believed her. The truth is I fell in love with both of them. David brought Graham to an opening I had in Washington, DC. David was, of course, charming as usual, impeccably dressed. Tall, thin, handsome. He was a scientist and worked for the government, but he seemed so sweet, so human. It was wonderful to watch him with Graham.

I could see right away what a smart little boy Graham was, and creative. I knew that I could give him something he was missing—not just a mother, but maybe a way of looking at the world. I bought him his first camera when he was seven, and he took pictures of other kids. He took pictures of me and David. And later we got him the video camera. Made sure he had something to occupy himself, help him understand the world around him and make use of it.

My work began selling well and I had money coming in and was able to get a bigger studio. I had work bought by the National Gallery, in London. It was right around then that David asked me to marry him, and that's when my mother said, Don't do it. You've got your career, you don't need anybody to look after you. But that was precisely why I *did* marry David! Unlike her generation, I was getting married by choice. I didn't need a man to support me. I could do whatever I wanted, and I wanted a family—one that I didn't need to start from scratch. I didn't want to take time out of my career to be pregnant and have a baby, and here was a child I could help out, because he needed a mom.

Later, when we would go to my mother's house in Connecticut for Thanksgiving, she fell in love with little Graham too. That's the way it was. He wasn't shy then. He was my little protégé, learning everything there was about how film worked and the visual world. And he was his father's son—learning everything about battles and strategies and looking at the world from a scientific distance. David worked for BAE Systems as a military aerospace strategist, based just outside of Washington in Virginia. But he was a simple man at heart, with good taste. He still loved to set up the telescope in the yard, and we would all lie out there together looking at the stars. Graham loved that most of all. He would ask millions of questions about how far away the planets were, was there life out there, how did light travel. It was only natural that he became who he was. Mechanically inclined, an artist, a boy who looked at the stars. Someone who thought about war and life and death.

I wish he'd never had to think so deeply about these things. We thought he was in good hands with Dr. Adams and on the new prescription. We thought the art helped his healing. The work he made . . . beautiful stuff, I have to say—even though I'm biased. The lawyer for the other family wanted to have his camera taken away permanently as part of the conditions of his probation, but of course, that was absurd. There was no way that was going to happen, I mean, I really put my foot down on that, and we had the lawyers to make sure he got out of there without some humiliating damaging sentence. He was a child! Sixteen is still a child! People don't know what they're doing at sixteen. If anything, the fact that he was trying to make art from a bad situation—I mean, that his initial response was to turn something terrible into something he could understand—was the most human thing that came from all of it.

Anyway, this new work had a maturity to it I don't think I've ever seen in a young artist. Especially the work he did in Rockland. Scenes from bridges, long camera shots with the telephoto lens. Things you can barely make out but that seem intimately familiar. Interviews with people intercut with digital feedback. It's all very exciting.

I think Graham had been a lonely kid this past year and he needed to process and understand what he went through. I think that was true the last year in Virginia too. I won't have people saying it was the art—that it was the art that caused all our sorrow. The truth is some of his art is the only consolation. It's the only thing that still remains.

AMANDA RICHARDS

saw her waiting as usual in her black jeans, that alert, funny, "I'm about to be in trouble" look on her face. "Tate!" I called to her, and she looked up and grinned sheepishly, walked in, and sat down as I shut the door. This was becoming a pretty common ritual with Ms. Tate.

I try to be a good example, but my office is pretty cluttered. They keep us busy at RHS and I had stacks of folders nearly dwarfing my desk. I always kept a jar of black licorice candy out for students, which for some reason was still three-quarters full.

"Tate, how's things?" I asked, and then went on without waiting for her usual smart-aleck answer. "I got this report here from your social studies teacher that says you've already missed six classes this quarter. What's up, girl?"

"Six classes? Sure you're not talking about my sister?"

"Ha! C'mon, don't give me that line again. I mean it, what's up? You're a straight-A student at risk of failing because of absences, detentions, and mouthing off. Doesn't quite make sense somehow. What can we do to fix it?"

She shrugged. "It's sixth period. Sometimes I take a long lunch."

I laughed. "Oh, I hear you, sometimes I want to take a long lunch too, but you know what?"

"What?" Tate asked.

"I don't."

Tate didn't know what to say for once. She smiled awkwardly and shrugged. I really liked this kid. She was one person who I thought about when the last bell rang. Wondered how she was doing and if she was going to make it out of Rockland High okay.

I leaned in close to her and whispered. "I'm going to tell you a secret," I said. "Everyone kinda hates high school. Unless they are a little bent. But once you're out, you're out, and it's a whole new world. You fail social studies, I mean, you do something stupid and just stop showing up, and you're gonna miss getting to that new world fast. You'll end up trapped somewhere you can't stand for even longer. Does that make sense?"

She rolled her eyes. I'd been telling her similar things last year too, until she came in with a list of successful high-school dropouts and handed it to me. "I hung this over my desk at home," she'd said. "Thought you might want a copy." Still, I wasn't about to give up trying. I got it about why she didn't want to be in school. She wanted to live in the world instead of sit at a desk. And she didn't know why she had to show up at all if she was getting good grades. And nobody had yet been able to make her see the logic in it. I also knew Tate got high, which, honestly, as long as she still did her work and didn't become a slacker, I didn't really care that much about. The thing I wanted her to do was show up. I wanted her to pass. I'd seen enough kids go through the system, and seen enough friends still working at Pizza Hut, to know that there were plenty of ways some seemingly innocuous drug could drag you down, but Tate's problem was being there at all.

"Well, look," I told her. "Whether it makes sense or not, promise me you'll go to class tomorrow. Okay?"

"Okay," she said. She looked up and nodded at me. "All right."

Tate left the office but lingered around outside. She really didn't want to go back to class—there were only fifteen more minutes anyway, and she could just as easily study a little right now by herself. And besides, something about hanging around Richards's office made her feel more relaxed. Syd liked Richards because she often saw her smoking on the way from the parking lot to the school, had a loud musical laugh that you could hear in the hallways, and wore black skinny jeans every day. Jeans and a pretty designer blouse. You could tell she didn't want to dress up at all.

And Tate could easily picture her wearing black lipstick

and a ball-chain necklace back when Richards was in high school herself. Now the woman wore a small string of pearls every day, but Syd considered it just a professional costume. She knew that Ally actually admired the pearls and blouse—tried to dress like that herself. Ally described her as "caring but professional," and Syd had to admit it was a good description. There was something about Richards that both girls liked.

Syd sat on the floor across the hall, where she could still look through the door. She watched Richards pull a file out of her drawer and look at it.

Principal Fitzgerald peeked his head into her office. And Syd watched from the hallway—waiting for him to tell her to get back to class—but he didn't seem to see her at all.

"Still pondering the fate of Tate?" he asked her.

Richards looked up. "She's a good kid, Dan," she said.

"That's the attitude we hired you for, Mandy."

"She *is*, though. I really think she could go on to a top ten. If something besides skateboarding could hold her interest for more than a week and she'd get herself to classes." She played absently with her pearls as she looked back down at the file. "Her standardized-test scores are high. Her teachers say this kid could be half there or dominate the class, bringing in all kinds of information or doing special reading or extra-credit projects. She's smart as hell. And she's always got that joke, 'You must be thinking of my sister,' when she's getting in trouble or getting particular praise. She's an interesting kid. Mercurial."

Syd could feel her heart beating harder listening to their conversation. She wanted to hear more and wanted to get up and leave before they said anything that might be upsetting or weird.

Fitz put his hand on the doorframe and leaned there. "Yeah," he said. "Her best friend Declan—maybe he's her boyfriend—has the same attitude. Kid's an incredible wiseass but clearly headed to Harvard. He's one of those geniuses who goes on to be a professor or gets scooped up to work on a government project. I wish they could be like their friend Becky. She's such a sweetheart, never in trouble."

"C'mon, Dan, it's harder for some people to pull off that intellectual rebel thing. Declan gets away with more because he's a boy. Becky has a little more poise for some reason, I suspect 'cause she gets a little more parenting. But Tate's got a lot of pressure. Hell, you know it's still a harder world for girls, and for some reason this kid with everything going for her is making it even harder on herself."

"And she's been making it harder on herself for years," Fitzgerald said.

"Anybody ever have a nice long talk with her parents?" Richards asked.

He shook his head and laughed. "If we could track them down," he said, and Syd felt butterflies in her stomach and the hair on the back of her neck go up as he talked about her parents. "Funny family," he said, scratching his head. "Never available. Rarely home. Her father's a builder. Salt-of-the-earth, back-country Mainer who made good. But y'know, sometimes even *I* can barely understand what he's saying. Accent so thick. The money comes from her mother's side, and that family owns half the state. Apparently they met when Mrs. Tate was home from college and he was doing some work on one of her parents' houses in Kennebunk. Or that's the gossip, anyway. Can't say I've been able to have a decent conversation with either one of them. Even back when Tate started that fire in the chemistry lab freshman year. I told them about it—the mother said, 'I see,' and a week later we had an anonymous gift for state-of-the-art lab equipment. But no change in the kid's behavior at all."

Richards shook her head. "That is the last thing in the world a kid like that needs. No consequences."

"Tell me about it," Fitzgerald said. "Between her and Declan we got just about no authority. It's hard to tell kids their grades will suffer if they screw off when the two of them are like the poster boy and girl for the benefits of having an attitude problem. Sure to be valedictorian and salutatorian—one or the other of them, and they're both little pains in my ass. Never seen anything like it."

"Trick is to keep them busy," Richards said. "Find a way to direct them, maybe."

"Well, that's true for Declan," Fitzgerald said. "Soon as the Model UN or chess club starts he's out of everyone's hair for a while and his detentions go down. But Tate? She's a special case. You'll see, Mandy, you'll see."

GRAHAM

00:00–13:42—Swing set
15:04—Cheerleading practice
18:51—Pine Grove Inn

Dear Lined Piece of Paper,
If they would let me stay home from school, I could get so much done! Already in the days since we've moved here I feel like I am on to something that's made me feel better than ever. It might be the drugs, sure, of course it could be the new drugs, especially given the fact that I've decided to adjust my own dosage! Not sure how Dr. Adams calculates these things but I was reading online and actually nothing major will happen to my liver if I take even four times *as much as they have me on. That means FOUR TIMES as relaxed. And FOUR TIMES as focused and FOUR TIMES better at getting everything done. So it might be the drugs but I think it's actually a whole*

new way of thinking about life!

I always believed it was best to see life from a distance, record it from a distance. And then watch it. We think we remember the way things are but we don't. That's why I don't even understand why I'm supposed to go to Dr. Adams. If he wants to know what happened he can just look at the footage. How am I supposed to talk about what I remember from years ago? Those things might not be accurate. Anyway, now I think I can get it right. I just need the perfect subject. I need the perfect character. I need someone who is brave and sweet and full of life, like Eric! I need a partner! And I know just the person. I don't know how I'll be able to put the camera down to go to school. But I figure I can get myself a smaller camera. Something tiny I can carry on a lanyard. Something people won't even notice. I'm not just trying to document my life. I'm trying to make sure I know who I am. And that when that moment comes again I'll be able to capture it perfectly. The problem with people as far as I'm concerned is they make up these phony personas. They walk around trying to make sure no one knows who they are—wearing whatever everyone else does, listening to whatever music is on the radio, but who are they really? They create whole fake versions of themselves for Facebook.

But on film—in the way I film them—there is a point where the facade breaks down, where you can see who they really are. What I'm giving people is a gift! And it's a gift I want for myself too! I want to know who I am. I don't think I've ever felt all that scared—shy, yes; pathologically shy, maybe, according to some— but scared? No way. Maybe someday I'll be able to scare myself, but so far it hasn't happened. When it happens I'll have it on film, that's for sure. I'll be able to see exactly what it looks like when whatever facade I've created for myself breaks down. Even if I don't know it's there. There's something inside of me and I feel like I am closer to getting to it than I've ever been before. Four times closer. LOL.

The main thing now is I need more money so I can do all this stuff without asking Dad and Kim to buy me equipment. Fortunately due to my superior reasoning (FOUR TIMES BETTER REASONING SKILLS) I've worked out THE PERFECT WAY to make some cash. I've set up a PayPal account and also an Amazon wish list so that people who download my films can pay me directly or buy me what I need and then just ship those things to me. You would not believe how interested people are in my films. It's amazing to me that I'm not already some kind of international superstar. I am like Quentin Tarantino and Stanley Kubrick all rolled into one.

So anyway, Kim is home all day but she's in her studio working and she has never once brought in the mail that I know of. So no one will know if I get packages or not. When I finish this project it will all make sense to everyone. Especially to me. I will understand things the way I couldn't before.

Between "finding my calling," as Dr. Adams would say, and working on the Austin Healey, I think life in Rockland is shaping up to be okay. And the neighbors! Beautiful Tate! I want to talk to her. I want to see her. I want to make her the star of all my films!!

ALLY

We were baking muffins together, which I have to admit only happened when Syd was high and in a good mood and there wasn't already a lot of junk food in the house. She'd convince me to make them and then we'd hang out in the kitchen. I guess it was one of the rare times we got along these days. And even though I didn't like her getting high all the time she could be silly and fun to be around when it was just the two of us.

Anyway, so there we were at the counter and we saw him from the window.

"You going to invite your crush over?" Syd asked, grinning at me.

I shrugged but before I could say anything she had opened the kitchen window and was yelling. "Hey! Justin Bieber, you wanna hang out?"

He looked up and I tried to push my hair away from my

face but my hands were all covered with flour and I got it in my hair and he started laughing.

"My sister has something for you," she said, and then started laughing as well. Great, I thought, she's going to be so stoned she'll embarrass me. Like the time she thought it would be a good idea to invite Declan and Becky over for a dinner we made together and then before we could eat she insisted we listen to the same four lines of a song she liked over and over and over again. Because it was "so cool."

But it was too late; Graham walked up the back steps and came right into the house.

"Looks like *you're* having a fun time this afternoon," he said. I could feel my face flush.

He took the mixing bowl and wooden spoon from my hands and started stirring. And I sat on the counter watching him.

Syd took the bowl from him, set it on the table, and became her usual bossy self. "Sit down," she told him. "I want to read your palm." She grabbed his hand and held it in her lap.

Syd of course did not know how to read palms at all. This was just the way she flirted with boys. If they were dumb, she read their palms; if they were smart, she'd challenge them to a game of anagrams.

"Or maybe you'd like to play anagrams instead?" I said to Graham. I never really got why they liked it—that game where you rearrange letters in a word. She and Declan played it all the time and it had them rolling on the ground laughing. By doing the palm-reading thing, she was telling me she thought Graham was dumb, but she was also getting to touch him, which I was sure she wanted. I sat down next to them.

"Oh, do you know how to play anagrams?" Syd said, stroking his palm lightly.

Graham said, "Ah . . . I kinda do, actually."

"Okay, we'll start with Eiffel Tower," Syd said. "Go."

He stared for a while and then asked for a piece of paper. She grinned a triumphant sort of grin and actually placed his hand into mine. Then she got up and sat on the counter, humming and mixing the batter, laughing to herself.

It felt good to hold his hand. It was wide and strong and his fingers were long and beautiful. I thought about him working on his car. "I don't really know how to read palms," I told him. "But I can tell we're all going to be friends." I looked up and smiled and he nodded, his face flushed. Now he really did look nervous, shy. I felt my stomach flutter.

"I better finish making these," I said, going to the counter and taking the bowl out of Syd's hand.

"You sure are an interesting girl," he said, and his eyes were shiny, gleaming beneath the yellow kitchen lights as dusk fell outside.

SYD

I had just a few hits of the bowl on my way home with Declan and Becky and was suddenly feeling very in the mood for some sister time in the kitchen and I didn't have to wait long. When I got home Ally was already standing at the counter, looking at a recipe book and twirling her long blond hair absently around her finger.

"Graham's coming over," she said. "I invited him over to make muffins with us."

"Oooooh. You're really making the moves on your crush," I said.

"Stop it, Syd. He's new here and we're his neighbors and we should be nice to him."

"Fine by me," I said. "As long as you're baking."

I reached into the bowl of blueberries and ate a few and she slapped my hand playfully.

We watched Graham lope across the driveway into our

backyard and up the steps and then he knocked.

"Hi!" Ally said, opening the door for him. I saw how he looked at her, that way some guys had where they were totally captivated by her homespun New England princess ways. And it made me smile. He looked like kind of a dork next to her, but he was also painfully good-looking.

"You wanna help mix the batter?" Ally asked.

"Yeah," he said. "Sure. Ah, could I use the bathroom for a minute?"

"I'll show you where it is," I told him. "You kinda got to go through a construction site. To get to it." Ally looked up at me sharply. She didn't like me saying anything negative about our house, but it was true, Dad's tools were everywhere and I'd rather say it myself than hear someone else point it out.

He followed me though the living room and out to the front hall. I sat on the piano bench while he went into the bathroom. He didn't shut the door. And then I heard a faint scraping, crunching sound. I wondered what he could be doing. I tiptoed into the hallway and peered around the corner. In the reflection of the mirror, I could see him cutting up a white pill. There were three other pills laid out on a hand mirror he'd clearly found in the cabinet.

"What are you doing?" I asked him.

He turned around, startled. "I . . . this . . ." He handed me a prescription bottle. "This is my anxiety medication," he said. "Sometimes when I feel nervous I, ah . . . snort it.

Because it, ah . . . it works faster."

I took the bottle and it was indeed a prescription made out to him. The pills also looked the same as the ones in the bottle. I stared at him. I felt kind of sorry for him, but it was also too weird. This kid was into some things I couldn't quite understand. Part of me wanted to understand them a lot better and part of me wanted him to leave.

"My sister really wouldn't like that," I told him.

"No," he said slowly, looking deeply into my eyes. "She seems very different from you."

"It's okay," I said. "I won't tell her."

ALLY

Since he hung out with me while I was baking, I guess it was my turn to hang out with him while he tinkered with his car. Or that's what I told myself when I wandered over to his garage and poked my head in. He smiled and waved for me to step inside and look at the Austin. I was impressed with how much he knew about fixing things, about technical stuff and engines. Not that I found any of it interesting myself. But I liked to watch him work.

It was one more thing that made it obvious Syd was exaggerating when she told me he was using drugs. I told her to mind her own business and not be a gossip. Besides, he might just be tired or stressed out, and lots of people needed to take drugs for ADHD and things like that. Then she told me she'd seen him *snorting* drugs when he was over at our house. She said she told him she wouldn't tell me, but I guess either jealousy or real concern made her do it. I thought her whole act was just really sad. Some attempt to get attention and make me not trust him at the same time.

Standing out there with him while he worked, watching how serious and focused he was, I knew Syd was exaggerating. He didn't act like Syd and her friends—laughing all the time and lying around listening to Death Cab and stuffing their faces with Doritos.

Graham glanced up from the engine and brushed his hair out of his eyes. "Whatcha thinking about?" he asked.

"My sister."

"What about her?"

"She thinks you're using drugs," I blurted out.

He put down his tools and came and stood in front of me. Wiping his hands off on a towel.

"She's right. I am."

I shrugged awkwardly, waiting for him to tell me some secret.

"I need them to concentrate and to not be anxious."

"That's what I told her," I said, and felt a flood of relief in my stomach.

He looked at me and his eyes were so blue and beautiful. He looked so sad and I felt that familiar flutter. Then he reached out his hand and I took it. I had the sudden desire to take care of him. I wanted people to know who he really was.

"I like Syd," he said. "She's fun. But I don't want her coming between us."

I smiled. "Don't worry. She won't."

BECKY

My mom called up to my room, and I ignored her, because I was writing code. It was one of those days where I would be wide-awake first thing in the morning with about a million ideas. And today I hadn't even gone down for breakfast before getting right to it. The thing I love about coding is that you are building a whole world, a whole architecture, making something totally new. It seems like gibberish to other people, but really it's very straight-forward.

I heard my mom call again and finally tore myself away from the computer and turned around and shouted, "What the hell? WHAT?!" just as the door was opening.

Tate peeked her head in, and my mom's voice yelled up the stairs, "I said, 'Tate's here!'"

I rolled my eyes and Tate laughed, came in, set her skate-board down, and then flopped on my bed. "Thanks, Mom!" I yelled back.

"Oh my God," Tate said. "You've been up all night being a super nerd again, haven't you? I swear, Becks, you are going to be awash in piles of sea glass jewelry and strands of computer code. Have you even combed your hair this week? And maybe change out of your pajamas?"

"Just got up early," I said distractedly, turning back to the computer. "I'll be done soon. Check this out."

"What the hell is it?"

"I'm building an app that finds and gathers all the internet radio stations with indie music on them."

"Doesn't something like that already exist?" she asked.

"Maybe."

"Why didn't you just buy it then?"

"I can do this for free," I told her.

"But it probably took you ten hours to write the program. That's a lot of free labor."

"Five hours," I said. "And I wanted to see if I could do it."

"What else were you doing?"

"I hacked into the public library and erased my fines."

"Why didn't you just take your books back?" She was being contrary—Tate loved this kind of sneaky stuff.

I shrugged and we started laughing. She said, "That's seriously cool, though. What else can you do?"

"I don't know. Whatever I want, I guess."

"You're something else, Becky. Most people would use those skills to do something that would benefit them more than finding places that are streaming Radiohead, or canceling a two-dollar fine."

"Baby steps," I told her. "After I get a sweet job with the NSA, then I can do some really cool stuff. I could be the next what's his name . . . that whistleblower guy who told everyone the government is spying on them."

"Edward Snowden?" she asked. "I'm pretty sure he can't come back to the country ever because they're going to put him straight in jail."

"Whatever. I'll be like that guy but without the having-to-go-to-jail part."

I could tell Tate was getting interested in writing code and hacking now that I said I could do something that was really against the rules with my skills.

"Can you show me how to do this stuff?"

"Last time I tried you got bored and wanted to go to the skate park."

"Yeah, but . . ."

"I know, it's pretty sweet, right? Pull up a chair. I'll teach you how to pick some digital locks."

Tate grinned. She seemed more motivated to do this than ever before. And I really didn't have a problem showing her or anyone else how to do it. It was so much fun. And usually she and Declan weren't interested in the things that I was. We were all friends, but sometimes I felt like she and Declan were going at twice the speed of everyone else around them, and it could be really annoying sometimes. They were super fun to smoke up with, but both of them could be a little high-strung or even preachy when they were just doing schoolwork. I liked writing code because it was relaxing. And honestly, it was one of those things that I just understood right away. And it was a thing that Tate and Declan had no idea about. Declan was even worse than Tate. He was big into his hippie idea that we should get rid of technology altogether.

I didn't know what exactly Tate would do with the things I taught her. She could be wild sometimes, but I'd known Tate all my life. She had been my friend since we were little girls, and she could be unpredictable. But there was one thing I did know—she was good at everything she did. I had no reason to think it would be any other way for learning how to hack.

SYD

t's not like me and Ally had some great relationship before Graham moved in next door. But things got weird after that. Really weird. Since Graham showed up, Allyson was always around. Suddenly she's just there. I'd look up at the skate park and there she was sitting on the rim. Watching us with that cute sheepish look she used to have when we were kids. That almost never happened before. I can probably count on one hand the number of times she'd come with me to skate—and usually it's to guilt me into going home and doing homework, which I have to say worked. I mean it would make me mad that she was just sitting there quietly exerting her goody-goody power over me, but it did make me go write papers I needed to hand in. But that day I remember it was just whacked-out. I thought she was supposed to be at work! Anyway, I rolled my eyes and waved to her—didn't want to be rude. But then the next time I went up the arc she was gone.

And again another time—I thought she was out with her friends after school. Dad was gone as always down by the harbor and Mom was God knows where—off to some Rah-Rah-Rockland event—and I thought I had the room and Declan all to myself.

The autumn sun was shining in the window, the air was cool and crisp, warm light spilled across the bed, and I had unbuttoned the top button of his jeans. He slid his thigh between my legs and pressed against me and pulled my shirt up over my head. His breath was sweet and smoky and I pulled him tighter to me and then . . .

Ally barged into the fucking room and just stood there with her mouth open in shock!

"Ugh!" I shouted, leaning over and grabbing my shoe and hurtling it at the door just as she shut it.

"What?" Declan asked. "God, chill, baby."

"Nothing, never mind."

He tried to kiss me again, but I just laid my head on his chest. Ally ruined the mood. I should have known something was up right then. I should have figured out why she was interrupting me, why she was hanging around. Why we seemed to be getting closer and yet more angry and annoyed with each other. It was like I could *feel* her feelings for Graham and they were somehow pulling me closer to him too.

But it would take another few weeks for me to put it together. Graham provided both the problem and the answer. Like I said before, he brought us together in a way we hadn't been since we were very, very little girls.

ALLY

*N*EVER. Never in the nine months that I worked at Pine Grove had Syd ever showed up to say hi. It was a thing I dreaded—and I had imagined many times the mortifying embarrassing moment when Syd stopped by in her strange clothes with her hair tangled, talking loud with her headphones on, not caring at all about other people's peace and quiet or whether or not this was a place of business. And then finally she did it. I was sitting down at the front desk, thank God, so she didn't have to go looking for me somewhere, which I imagine would have been a nightmare.

At least she kept her voice down. "I think you better watch out for Graham," she said. "He's not some sweet broken doofus from the suburbs—he's all kinds of fucked-up."

"I think I can make up my own mind about these things," I told her.

"Ha!" she said. "As. If. If I wasn't here you'd already be dead."

This is just the type of melodramatic thing she says. "You'd be dead" or "I'd rather be dead" or "This is the worst thing in the entire world" or "I hate/love that more than anything in the world."

Then to make her point she brought up her stupid list of ways she's "saved" me, which started with a trip our day school took—how was I supposed to know some kinds of toads are poisonous?—and ended with her writing the personal essay part of my Emerson application. Which I did not even ask her to do and how can we know that has anything to do with whether I'll get in or not? I was completely exasperated with her.

Finally I just said, "What the hell do you want?"

"I want you to stay away from Graham! How many ways do I have to say it? He did some creepy thing with Becky— filming her and writing about it in a little notebook—and I think he's got some weird fucked-up stuff going on. I've been watching him."

"It sounds like YOU have some weird stuff going on," I told her. "It sounds like *you're* the one people should watch out for, spying on him. Maybe *he* should watch out for *you*."

She slapped her forehead dramatically. Another thing she always does.

"Listen," I said, quietly and reasonably. "Why don't you just try being honest for once in your life and admit that you don't want me around him because you've got a crush on him."

"That's not true! I totally do not have a crush on him.

C'mon, have you seen Declan Wells? Do you think I need someone like Graham when I've got Declan? Hello? Declan Wells? Dec. Lan. Wells?"

"You're jealous," I said simply. "I don't know exactly how or why but you are."

She said, "Just try to use your head, okay?" *Another* thing she says all the time to me: "try and use your head"—as if I'm a complete idiot. I was starting to lose my patience.

"And you try to calm down," I whispered fiercely. "You can't come to my work. You may get away with everything at home, but you can't bring your weird problems here. Okay? Can't you just wait until I get home to talk about this stuff? Why don't you listen to anyone EVER?"

"Why doesn't anyone listen to ME?" She actually looked pained, like she might cry. It was the first time since we were children that I saw her look so vulnerable. And that of course is my weakness. No matter how hard it is to deal with her, I always have compassion for her in the end. Somewhere deep down I know she means well. I wanted to listen to her, I wanted to work it out. But this was my job. She could disrupt our home life, but she couldn't come around disrupting my job.

"All right. All right," I said, coming around the desk and putting my arm around her. "We'll talk about this at home, okay? We can talk all about it. I'm serious."

"Forget it, Ally." Her face was calm again and she looked around as if she didn't know why she was there either. She started putting her headphones back on.

I reached out and brushed her hair out of her eyes. Even though we live in the same room in the same house we barely touch each other. We don't usually hug. We don't dance or wrestle or put our arms around each other anymore. She pulled away and in that moment she looked like she totally understood about why she had to go.

"I'm sorry," she said to me. And that was another first.

SYD

Richards called me into her office *again* and I swear if it was anyone else I just would have skipped it entirely. I was really beginning to be sick of all this go-to-the-office bullshit. They could threaten me all they want. I have to do this or I have to do that. But really, what are they going to take away from me? I am second in the class behind Declan and if he keeps on smoking weed the way he does, I'll be valedictorian by senior year. Even if I stop going to detention what are they going to do? Kick me out of school? And find someone else to win the Odyssey of the Mind competition for them all? Hardly. This stupid school owes me more than I owe it. Rules are for people stupid enough to follow them.

So anyway talking to Richards is not that bad because I think she actually gets all that stuff. She's not like other teachers. With her weird licorice candy and her cigarette breath and her funky shoes, she kinda stands out. I bet she's got tattoos underneath those pretty blouses she wears. Richards is cool. And if I ever doubted it, that day she called me in to talk about my "attitude" confirmed it.

"Tate, you are killing me," she said as she shut the door. "Are you trying to kill me? I swear you are."

"I assume this is about Letorno's class?"

She raised her eyebrows and sighed heavily. "Oh, great. Is there some *new* report I *haven't* gotten on you yet?"

"Maybe," I said, and laughed a little.

She shook her head. "No," she said. "This isn't about Letorno. It's about skateboarding between classes, not wearing your shoes, and taking down flags that are hanging in the classroom. I have six different reports today *alone* about you skateboarding in the halls, skating on the front steps at lunch, and smoking on school grounds. Once again, girl: that board is supposed to be: In. Your. Locker."

I shrugged.

"Listen. We got just a little more time to get through and then I swear to God, Tate, I swear. Look at me. After that you can go be a professional skater or an astrophysicist or whatever the heck it is you want to be, but here at RHS you gotta. Chill. Out."

"Why?" I didn't mean to sound like a snot or to just be contrary. I really was just curious. "I mean why do I have to stop all the things I do?"

"Because when you apply to schools you will have a

disciplinary record that makes you look like someone who can't handle the organization and pressure of academia. You'll look like someone very inconsistent—why do you *think*? I'm not worried that Letorno is pissed about something or that you might fall and get hurt boarding in the halls. I don't care what you wear or if you don't wear shoes. I don't care about that stuff. I *know* you're competent at what you do. I know you understand things really quickly and you want to go outside instead of reviewing things in class. But I just care about you being able to leave Rockland and go where you'll be *happy* and get a good education and be around people who will appreciate you for who you are."

I nodded. No one had said anything like that to me and it actually made sense and I really did want Richards to feel better. I did. But I honestly didn't know if I could do what people at school wanted. That was Ally's job.

I shrugged. "I'm not one of those girls who does what everybody wants," I tried to explain, and for some reason my voice came out all hoarse and weird.

Richards nodded. "Yeah," she said. "Exactly. I see what's going on. There's the problem right there. Thinking that there are *kinds of girls* who do *kinds of things*. Let me ask you something: You might not be doing what other people want, but are you actually doing what *you* want?"

I shrugged again.

She said, "You know, Tate. There are no *kinds of girls*. That's something people make up to get women to behave in certain ways. Something people make up so they can control what you do."

"The slut or the virgin," I said. I knew about that stuff. I knew there were double standards. Big deal. I didn't think I really had any part in those things.

"Right," she said. "There's lots of stupid ideas about girls, but we don't have to pay attention to them, because they don't make sense. And the more we ignore them, the more we tell people they're wrong when they try to tell us there are two ways of being, the freer we all get. Got it? This attitude of yours doesn't make a lot of sense either. You're not going to become some obedient, weak person if you just follow some of the school rules so you can get into a good college. You'll still be yourself. You use what the school gives you to get somewhere else. Hell, Tate, I don't think you could get a bad grade if you tried. But you can sure make yourself get stuck here by other means, and you seem to be working hard at it. You don't have to wrestle with being a certain way, with being *good* or *bad*. You're just who you *are*."

"Okay. But who I *am* is someone who skips classes and skateboards in the hall."

"Look," Richards said. "You don't have to prove anything to anyone. I understand that you have different feelings at different times. I'm just saying, don't let some weird idea about how girls are supposed to act dictate the way you live. You don't have to be a tough guy all the time. You get what I'm saying?"

"I guess."

She sighed and offered me a Twizzler. When I declined, she said, "Take it! For God's sake, it's an acquired taste. You have to at least *try* it!"

"You know everyone hates black licorice, right?"

"Because they're philistines," she said, winking. I loved that she always used that word. I never knew what it meant until I met her.

I took the licorice from her, took a tiny bite, and smiled politely even though it tasted terrible.

"Now, seriously. Listen. And listen good," Richards said. She leaned in close. "There used to be a time when girls weren't allowed to get an education at all. Women weren't allowed to go to college; and when they were, they had to go to segregated schools and study things like home economics. We only got the vote about one hundred years ago."

"Your point?"

"My *point*?" She looked really annoyed.

"Okay. Okay," I said. "I get your point."

"If you want to be the tough girl, you go out there and you rule. You understand me? You go get the best grades and work hard and cruise your way to making a real change in the world. Not this stupid part you're playing, being the bad girl—okay? There are *not* two sides to this equation. It's one problem we all gotta solve together."

It kind of shocked me to hear her say it so plainly. Or

I guess even say it. No one had ever talked to me like that before. I felt goose bumps up and down my arms.

She looked at me for a long time. "Oh, Jesus, just give me that thing back." She took the licorice out of my hand and chucked it in the garbage. I had taken a kind of nanobite out of it. "You kids have no taste." She laughed. "Are we good, Tate?"

I smiled at her. "Yeah," I said. "I think we are. I'll . . . I'll think about it."

I walked out of there and for some reason all I wanted to do was go talk to Ally. I mean I suddenly wanted to grab her hand and run with her out into the woods and tell her she didn't have to be the way she was. Neither of us did. I thought of going home and rearranging our room— finding some stuff we both cared about to put up on the walls instead of having it be this demilitarized zone down the middle and warring posters and objects in every corner of the room.

I remembered how it was when we started school. She just became obsessed with the way people thought about her. How she dressed. What boys said to her. How they looked at her. She was always very pretty and dudes said some fucked-up stuff to her even when she was in grade school. She started getting really self-conscious about being good. She was already like this, of course—always being good trying to get Mom and Dad's attention or cleaning up their messes.

But I realized now that school really was the key. She somehow shrunk when we got there. Became afraid to talk in class. Almost like she was afraid to be smart. All she wanted to do was look like some perfect, clean, wholesome, rich, untouchable girl like out of an L.L.Bean catalog. And I think that's what made me want to just tear everything apart. I think that's what made me want to say no to everyone and be above all their bullshit by never listening. It was like I was trying to save Ally by being the anti-Ally, but I was wrong too. Just before I went in to see Richards, I'd been thinking that rules are for people stupid enough to follow them. And she had basically told me the same thing! That there aren't any rules for how girls have to be.

I remember thinking, This will bring us together. This will bring me and Ally together.

I decided not to stay at school that afternoon and just go to the skate park by myself. I had that great Death Cab song in my head. "I want to live where soul meets body. And let the sun wrap its arms around me." I waited until I got outside to put the board down and my headphones on. Then I cruised along the curb. The wind in my hair. I had on my black T-shirt and hoodie and my skinny jeans with the hole in the knee. My slip-on Vans were solid on the board and I felt great. I felt for a moment like I didn't need to worry about anything. About Ally or about myself. Maybe we had a lot to teach each other. Maybe if each of us changed a little neither of us would have to be so extreme. There was no reason for us to be separate. Now that we were older and could take care of ourselves.

I wish I could go back to that feeling. I wish that feeling had been true.

When I got to the skate park, Graham was sitting in his car smoking. Apparently he hadn't officially started school or was given some time off—still checking things out. That was weird, but sometimes kids just checked out a school for a few days before their parents made a decision about whether they would go. Especially kids like Graham whose parents could probably send him to any prep school they wanted.

He had the top down and had his feet propped up on the dash and he had headphones on too. I skated up and he acted startled, even though he was watching me the whole time.

"Is it Saturday?" I asked him.

"It must be," he said. "We're not in school."

"Becky said you made another movie of her."

"I did. And I'm making one of you right now," he said.

I looked closely at his headphones and realized there was some kind of tiny camera attached to the one over his right ear. He wasn't listening to music at all. He'd been filming people driving and walking by.

"I don't want to be in your movie," I said.

"Okay, cool." He took the headphones off and set them down on the seat. He clicked off a tiny button with his thumbnail.

When he looked up again without the camera he seemed just for a second afraid. Very afraid, like a little kid who was all alone. Then it passed over his face and was gone.

"Got any weed?" he asked.

"I wish," I said. "Declan's the source there. And he's got Model UN and then debate team after that."

"Isn't that weird?" Graham asked.

"What?"

"That like the school pothead is like the school valedictorian."

I shrugged. "I wouldn't call him the school pothead. I've spent a good deal of time in detention with some dudes who seem to have permanent brain damage. There's a lot of waking and baking going on."

"Huh." Graham nodded but it seemed like he wasn't really listening to me. "Want to try these?" He reached in his pocket and took out two pills.

"What is it?"

"One is Adderall and the other is Xanax," he said. "They're both pretty hefty dosages. You take them together."

"Are those your parents' prescriptions?"

He shook his head.

"What do they do?"

"Make you feel like you can do whatever you want for

as long as you want and nothing in the outside world can stop it."

I laughed. "I don't need a drug for that. I already feel that way."

"Okay." He shrugged, unconvinced. "But you could feel even more that way. Let me know if you ever want some."

I hesitated for a minute. I did want some. I generally did what I wanted, but with a lot of annoyance and interference from the outside world. "Is it okay to take them both at the same time?"

"I've taken two of the Adderall and three of the Xanax," he said. "It makes you feel like a champion, like you can do whatever you're good at nonstop for like a thousand years. And you understand everything better than you would otherwise."

"Everybody thinks they understand stuff better on weed too." I laughed. "But they don't."

"Yeah, but not with this," he said. "It's actually made to enhance your performance. Make you focus. And then the Xanax takes the edge off. It's just right."

"How did you get that stuff?" I don't know why I worried that Ally would ever want to be with this guy. If this was the way he acted, she would avoid him like the plague. This was not her kind of thing at all and people like this generally scared her.

"My doctor prescribed them to me." His pupils were very dilated and he was looking intently at me. I actually think if Richards and I hadn't had that talk I would have already swallowed the pills—maybe taken however many he gave himself. I would have felt like whatever he did I had to do more of and I had to do it better. I could actually see how fun it would be to take the stuff and then focus only on skating—just be free to be there all day and night—getting tricks right, not getting bored, being relaxed. But this time the voice that is usually Ally's in my head—the nitpicking nagging sister's voice—was my own.

Maybe I'd do it later but not now. Not just to prove something to him.

"Yeah. No thanks, maybe another time."

He said, "If you ever want to try it, let me know. I have an endless supply. We could take some and go driving in the countryside. It's really fun to drive on this stuff because you feel so relaxed and capable and you know you can go as fast as you want. I think you'd love it." He took out his phone and I thought he was texting something but then my phone rang. "That's my number," he said when I looked down at the screen.

"How did you get *my* number?" I asked.

"You gave it to me. Don't you remember?"

I didn't remember and it freaked me out. But then I thought maybe I did or maybe Declan did when he was showing him around school. This last theory seemed like it was probably right because the next thing he said was:

"Is Declan your boyfriend?"

I shrugged.

"Sometimes it's like you guys are joined at the hip and other times he's not around for like a week."

I said, "Declan is my friend."

"I want to be your friend," he said. "I miss my friend."

SYD

ecause I left school early and didn't have detention, I got
home around the same time as Ally. I was excited to talk
to her. When I got upstairs she was brushing her hair and
listening to this terrible crap. Amber Carrington. Some girl
who was on *The Voice*. She got famous from this sappy song
called "Stay." As usual Ally was singing along. I couldn't
decide if this was better than all the terrible Rihanna she
listened to or not. I watched her for a while. She was happy,
holding her hairbrush as if it were a mike and singing the
song with so much emotion, her head thrown back.

"Hey!" I said.

She turned around and dropped the brush, totally startled. I laughed.

"Argh! How many times do I have to tell you? Don't
sneak up on me!"

She thought I was doing it on purpose and I can't blame

her really because it's totally the kind of thing I would do on purpose.

"How was school?" I asked.

"Good."

"Do you have to work?"

"Why? Do you want the room to yourself? Is Declan coming over?"

"No," I said. "I thought we could hang out."

She looked at me warily and turned the music down.

"We," I said. "You and me. I'm serious."

"What do you want, Syd? I was going to bake muffins later anyway. You don't have to pretend to want to hang out with me to get some, you know I always give them to you."

"Hey. I'm serious," I said.

"Is something wrong?" She frowned and looked at me, worried.

"No!" I said. "Not at all. It's just . . . I was talking with Richards."

"I know, I heard you get called down to the office."

"Right. Whatever. Just listen to me, okay? I was talking with Richards and she had all this stuff to say about how girls think they have to act certain ways, like be good or bad, and I was thinking about us. I thought maybe . . . I thought maybe we should spend some time together. Because maybe we're making each other the way we are. Maybe we're not really opposites but we just think we have to be or something. I don't know."

"I've never thought I was any certain way," she said. "I'm just being myself."

"Right right right!" I said. "But when we act like ourselves, we're acting in some way that is expected of us and there are generally two ways that girls are expected to act, right? I don't know. I think I finally got it figured out."

"What out?"

"The way we are!" I said. "Like this." I grabbed her iPod off the speakers right in the middle of Amber Carrington's sappy melodic whining, "I want you to staaaaaaaayyyyy." And I took my iPod out and scrolled down to the Distillers' song "The Hunger." Brody Dalle belted out her raspy punk shriek over the screaming guitar and heavy drums. "Don't goooooooo!" she screamed.

"See?" I said. "It's the same song."

She had her finger in her ears, but she started to get a little smile on her face. "That is NOT the same song!" she yelled, laughing a little.

"It is though," I told her. "It's the same thing going on. And look around the room," I said. "The stuff we like is not all that different. We just like it served up in a different way."

"Are you really high?" she asked.

I turned down the music. "No," I said. "But I ran into Graham and *that* kid is on some serious drugs."

She frowned. "He's got a prescription for his learning disability," she said.

"How do you now that?"

"Because I was talking to him about stuff. About moving

and Virginia and starting school and all that. If you didn't have detention every night you might get here when he's working on his car after school and you could talk to him too."

"Okay. Well, anyway." I didn't want to get distracted by Graham again so I kept on talking about what was important. "What do you think about what I'm saying?" I jumped up on the bed and turned up the Distillers again and grabbed her hairbrush and screamed into it along with Brody Dalle. "Don't go!"

She laughed. "You sound like you did when we were little and Mom and Dad would go out for the night."

I nodded and started laughing too. "C'mon, Al, let's build a fort and get some ice cream. We're just fine without them."

She shook her head at me and looked like she was about to cry. Then finally she said, "Syd, you're nuts," and got up on the bed with me and we both started jumping and dancing and shouting, "Don't go!"

And I couldn't stop laughing. I was having fun with my sister for the first time in years and years. We didn't need to be apart at all. We could really be like this. I tore my Tony Hawk poster down from my side of the room and went over and hung it over her bed.

"Don't tell me you don't think he's hot!" I yelled over the music.

She rolled her eyes. "Please, Syd," she said in a mock-sophisticated tone that sounded just like our mom, "I may not skateboard but I'm not *blind*." She handed me a thumbtack and pulled the top of the poster up so it would be perfectly straight.

Then she went into her closet and she got out Sparkle Pig. The stuffed animal we used to fight over when we were little. He was a little pig in a T-shirt that had glitter writing on the front that said "Sparkle." She tossed him to me.

"Seriously?" I asked

"I know you said you hate him now. But, uh . . . actually . . . I know you don't."

I made Sparkle Pig dance up to her and scream "Don't go!" and then flopped down on the bed. "Sparkle Pig, you are mine," I said to him and set him on my pillow. "Mine and mine alone."

I tossed him back over to Ally, but he just landed on her bed.

"Ally, listen," I said. "I think you and I should really be unified. No more fighting. No more attitude. We'll be stronger that way. Richards is right."

I remember how she looked at me then; like she was scared and confused. She sat down on the bed and put her head in her hands. I thought she would be happy that I had figured some things out. I thought she would be happy I wasn't acting like a bratty little punk and wanted to hang out with her. But the way she looked . . . it was like I just told her she had a month to live.

"But we are together," she said. "Aren't we?"

ALLY

Syd came home late as always because she had detention and I was already doing homework in our room. Daddy had a meeting with some folks at the harbor and Mom was shopping.

When we were little kids and they would be gone for a long time, we used to make up plays. I would always be the princess and she would be the witch. Or I would be the damsel in distress and she would be the mad scientist. I would be Wendy and she would be Peter. The only time she wanted to be a good guy is when she wanted to be Pocahontas.

When our parents came home we'd show them the play we made up and they would laugh. One time when I was eight, they went away for the entire day to some boat auction and we made up a play about two orphans that had everything in it: songs, dancing, jokes, costumes. It was mostly Syd's idea. She was really good at coming up with characters. We went through our parents' closet and put on their clothes. Syd wore Dad's shoes with one of our princess dresses and clomped around and we fell on the floor laughing so hard.

I remember Mommy marveling at us: "How do you do those different voices?!" Sometimes I wished we could still play those games together.

Syd dumped her books on the bed and then opened the window and fished out a pack of cigarettes from the bottom drawer of our dresser.

"Can you stand by the window if you're going to smoke?" I asked her. I had long given up on telling her about lung cancer and the general grossness of smelling like an ashtray.

She moved closer to the window and didn't argue or have some snappy comeback, which is when I realized something was wrong. Syd rarely did anything you asked. Maybe for Declan and Becky, but not for me or Mom or Dad. She looked out the window into the little woods.

"You okay, sis?"

She exhaled a cloud of smoke and nodded, then shrugged. She went over to the speaker and took my iPod off right in the middle of Rihanna's "Stay" and then put hers on. Something with a lot of yelling.

"I saw that kid Graham over by the skate park," she said.

"Cute, right?" I ignored the fact that she just took my

music off because I was so used to it and because I honestly didn't care that much.

She looked up and grinned in spite of herself, gave a little nod.

"Cute, but weird," she said.

"I think he's just shy," I said. "I walked home with him the other day and he seemed all right."

"You did? What did he talk about?" she asked.

"Movies. How he spends more time on making them and working on his car than anything else. How he likes to build things. I had to ask him a million questions; otherwise I think he'd just walk along saying nothing, looking at everything. I think he really needed someone to talk to though, like he's looking for a friend. I guess things were rough when he was living in Virginia. He had this one best friend, Eric, and they made all these movies and then I guess Eric's parents sued his parents or something and now they don't even talk."

Syd's eyes grew wide. "Whoa, I wonder what Graham did."

She had that expression she gets when she's strategizing. I've seen it plenty, like when she's trying to figure out how to take just the right amount from the liquor cabinet without getting caught. Or how to sneak out to meet Declan. "You should try to find out what he did."

I sighed. "Maybe he didn't do anything," I told her. I came over and sat on her bed—something I rarely do, but I did it right then because I felt like we were really getting along.

She stubbed out her cigarette and then went into our bathroom to flush it.

When Syd is worried she tries to look tough, so I knew just by looking at her something was really bugging her. Not that I'd seen her worried too many times. She can go months without studying or read really upsetting things or see them on TV or listen to our parents argue and she never gets worried. I guess worrying is my job, so when I saw her eyebrows furrow like that I paid attention.

She said, "Doesn't Graham seem like the kind of kid who's going to come to school with a Bushmaster rifle? You know, the rich, white, spaced-out loner type? That's always the kind of kid who ends up really doing damage."

"You're the rich, white, spaced-out loner type," I said, and poked her in the side.

She laughed. "Yeah, well, takes one to know one I guess."

"You have a crush on him?"

She shrugged. "Do you?"

"Yeah," I said. "I guess I do."

She seemed so sad and resigned when she said it. And suddenly I thought, Wow, Syd's jealous of more than just my job. And she's trying to be good about it. I mean that really threw me for a loop, because Syd is, like, never jealous. Of anyone. Mean? Check. Snotty? Check. Competitive? Check. Check. Check. But jealous or insecure about a boy? And trying to be reasonable? Not my sister. As crummy as she could act sometimes, she never liked it when girls got all hung up on boys or fought over them. And she had never cared before about any boy I'd had a crush on. Didn't even pay attention to them. She always just thought they were nerdy or preppy or not her type. But this was not like her. It was confusing and honestly annoying. My feelings for Graham were strong. He wasn't some boy I just wanted to fool around with.

I told her, "I like him, Syd. Maybe he's more your type, but *I* actually like him. And you can't tell me who to date. Besides, you already HAVE a boyfriend."

"Declan is not my boyfriend," she said. "And that's not what this is about, you moron. Something's off about him. If anyone can tell, I can." She didn't sound angry, just really worried, and I couldn't tell if she was pulling my leg—somehow making fun of me.

"I'll make my own decisions," I said. And she looked shocked. "I'm my own person, Syd. You and I are not the same in any way. And we never will be. And besides, I'm older than you."

Syd may be smart but she is still immature. She's overly emotional. Sometimes you have to just tell her how things are. "You and I are not unified on this at all. And I'm not going to fight with you. We are not coming together on this."

She glared at me.

"No," she said. "You don't know how to fight. You just leave it up to me."

POLICE CHIEF CODY DALY

Well, it was terrible, but his dad was some bigwig up at BAE Systems. That place that makes drones for the war—surveillance drones I guess, some big technology firm. There were folks here who wanted him tried as an adult. He was lawyered up before he even left the hospital—he had a fractured collarbone, a cracked rib, some cuts and bruises. Split lip. He was practically untouched considering. Lawyered up and a juvenile, so his name never appeared in the papers. No one ever knew. The DA was fuming. Other parents were horrified. I mean, we had a real situation. And what could I do? I knew my place in that town like everyone else. Knew where the money was coming from. We didn't even call him into the station. We went by his house in an unmarked car as a courtesy.

But we already knew we didn't need to be sensitive with him. They had some hotshot psychologist come in and say that the reason he did what he did was because he was in shock. That he was trying to cope. They said what else did we expect from someone raised in a society with reality TV and Facebook and everybody being the star of their own little show? There was a lot of talk about ADHD and prescription pills and whether or not people are responsible for their actions under that kind of medication. What else did we expect from a society that rewards young men for speed and recklessness? There was a lot of talk about computer games and Second Life and the effects of too much soda drinking and everything else under the sun. What else did we expect? they kept asking. Not that.

When he couldn't be tried as an adult, we wanted him to have at least two years in juvenile detention. No dice there either. He got probation and mandatory counseling, and that, at least, the parents took seriously. Actually, I can't say they didn't take the whole thing seriously, really. I mean, who wants to know their kid did something like that? They had the best psychologists and psychiatrists and they made sure he got on different medication.

I learned something during that case. Something I'd been denying since I joined the force. I learned that when you're rich and white and your dad works for the biggest company in the region, you don't go to jail. Even when the whole town is calling for you to be locked up or worse; even when the whole town is shocked; even when you post your own video of the crime on YouTube—if you're that kid, you do not go to jail.

You get a new car and a new life in one of the prettiest

little towns in the northeast. I have to uphold the law. But I don't have to keep my mouth shut. And when I found out they moved to Rockland, I just sent a friendly note to my buddies on the force there. Thought they should maybe know who might be driving fast down their streets, who might be picking up passengers and taking them for a ride.

ALLY

It rained in the morning so I didn't ride my vintage blue Schwinn to school. But it had cleared up by the time school was over. The sun was shining through the leaves just starting to turn and the air smelled like pine and a subtle brackish breeze from the water. The streets were still wet and everything felt lush and alive. I turned onto Euclid Avenue where the sidewalk ended and stepped out onto the winding road that led up into our beautiful tree-lined neighborhood. The Austin Healey cruised up beside me and Graham leaned over the passenger-side seat and unlocked the door. His hair fell in his eyes and he brushed it back, smiled shyly. He threw his backpack into the tiny backseat. And leaned his head out the window. His hair fluttered in the light wind and I could see the square cut of his jaw and his nice straight teeth.

"You want a ride?" he asked.

I smiled. I did want a ride. I wanted to sit beside him and drive up around the crest of the hillside and look at the ocean with him. I wanted to feel the autumn wind in my hair too and see his profile as he drove and put the radio on and put my feet up on the dashboard. I wanted to do all those things.

"Were you at school today?" I asked. "I didn't see you."

"I took a personal day," he said. "Finally got the Austin moving again and my dad let me go to the DMV and get all the paperwork taken care of. Wanna get in?"

When he asked me just like that, it made my stomach flip-flop. He was so shy and the shyness was still visible in his eyes, but he was also relaxed and happy. I could see it. He looked excited and his eyes were shining, gleaming. He wanted to share this new thing with me. His new accomplishment. I knew it was a big deal for him to be driving again. I'd seen him working on the car for so long and so this was a monumental day really. The fact that he was driving at all and was excited to be out on the road and that he would ask me to be with him on such a special day made me feel light-headed. Made me catch my breath.

The only thing that made me hesitate was thinking about Syd. Even though she tried to deny it, Syd had this crush on him. I wanted that to matter—to make a difference to me—but right in those moments it didn't matter. I wanted to ride beside him and wear his jean jacket and help him adjust to life in Maine and go to the beach and watch the surf and hear the cracking of smooth round stones washing up onto the land with him. I wanted to lie beneath the pines where our backyards connected and look up through the branches at the stars.

And I wanted to kiss him. Not the boring kind of endless making out I always had to see when Syd had Declan over but a real kiss. A proper sweet kiss from this beautiful boy who had told me secrets and survived sadness and trouble and had eaten the blueberry muffins I baked and had rebuilt his own car. The boy whose eyes shone with excitement and a kind of expectation when he saw me. I wanted all those things.

"I would love a ride," I said, opening the car and slipping my backpack onto the floor. I got in and buckled my seatbelt and he smiled at me, and I was so happy. I was so happy right then all I could do was laugh.

SYD

was starting to feel sorry for the way I'd treated Ally these past few years. I knew I owed her more and I was trying to figure out some way to change things. I started thinking about when we were little. How cool she was when we were little kids. My best memory of her, my *favorite* memory of her, is when we built our giant Lego castle together. It took all day. I don't know where our parents were. I was sad and crying for Mom and looking for her all over the house. And Allyson got out the big tub of Legos and dumped them on the floor. I think I was four and she was six.

And she said, "Don't cry, silly. I'm your big sister so I can take care of you. Daddy is just working on the boat. He'll come back. Mommy will come back." And we played all afternoon together. We built the biggest most beautiful castle you'd ever seen.

And everything I wanted to do she said yes to. Maybe

that's why I like that memory so much. Because later she said no to just about everything. But then I remember I asked if we could stand on a chair and get the ice cream out of the freezer and eat the whole thing and she said yes. She said, We can do whatever we want if we stay in the house and don't get hurt.

I remember crying for a long time after we ate the ice cream because we were still all alone. And she kept looking at me and smiling and patting my back. Like some little blond angel who showed up.

She got all the blankets off our bed. She put the big comforter under the table and she put the sheets on top of the table so they hung down and made tent flaps. And then she got inside.

"Come on in," she whispered. "This is our secret fort." She brought all of our toys out and set them around the table to keep guard. "C'mon," she said. "It's going to be fun." And we climbed under the table.

It was so cool, even though I was afraid that our parents were gone. The fort was like our own little house. And we were making up our own rules. I crawled in and lay down and she sang to me until I fell asleep.

I loved Allyson. But I never understood why she didn't get angry at our parents for being gone. She didn't question anything. All she did was come up with solutions to fix things and make them better. Wait for our parents; listen to our parents. It was like her whole existence revolved around understanding what was going on with *them*, what *they* wanted, how to behave when company was there and how to be brave and cheerful when no one was there.

I used to think that she was always looking out for us. But then I had this realization that she put *everyone else* first. I started to think the real reason she took care of me was so that our parents wouldn't have to. And the way she never got mad—it was just too weird. She wanted me to behave myself so everyone would think we were the perfect family. So no one would ever doubt our parents. So no attention would be drawn to the fact that they were never there. Once I figured that out there was no way I was just going to be the good girl. I wasn't going to pretend I was happy when I wasn't. I wasn't going to act like everything was normal.

But she would explain things to me so that everything seemed fine even when I felt terrible. "Grown-ups have their own lives, silly." This is how all grown-ups are.

Once I had friends and not just Ally I realized that wasn't how most grown-ups were at all. Most people's parents were around and wanted to know where you were and what you were doing. Not just bring you to the harbor every month or so to stand on the dock and hand them tools, or bring you to some gala where you had to dress in a complete miniature replica of the dress your mother was wearing, right down to the pearl drop earrings and pearl necklace. Ally could do that stuff and still adore our parents. I couldn't. I just couldn't.

I don't want to think about how it turned out in the end. I don't want to be angry. I know now why she rejected me after I came home talking about Richards and how we should come together. I know now why it scared her. Even though Ally was a force she somehow knew I was the stronger of the two of us. I wish I had understood what was going on then.

I just want to remember her that day sitting in the little fort singing me to sleep, our breath sugary and sweet from the Cherry Garcia ice cream. Our Lego castle radiant in the sunshine that shone down from the beautiful skylight. Her hand in mine beneath the table. I want to remember her from a time when I loved how good she was instead of resented it.

I want to remember that I owe it to her to take care of her. I mean I think I learned that from her. I was trying to do the right thing. The thing she would have done.

She took care of both of us back when we needed it the most.

GRAHAM

Dear Lined Piece of Paper,

I can hardly believe how lucky I am sometimes. This town— this neighborhood—really is full of pretty girls, but the prettiest one of all was in my car yesterday. Smiling and riding along with her hair in the breeze. It is amazing to be out driving again, especially with her, and I know I'll soon be able to get out and do what I want. Drive fast. Drive all night, break out of this feeling like there's something hanging over my head.

I was telling her everything. I was telling her all about living in Virginia and my dad's work in surveillance and all about Eric. How we were going to be stars. She's so quiet and patient and sweet and she laughs at all my jokes and it's so good to have someone listen to me. Not listen like Dr. Adams but really listen. She told me all about her life too.

It's hard to keep straight what she said. I think it was mostly about sailing and some school she wants to go to but I can't remember the name of it or what she wants to study. I'll just watch the tape of it later though, so I don't need to remember. She told me she's going to bake me some more blueberry muffins. That part I do remember. She's the friendliest person I've ever met.

I think she is the exact right person for me to be with. Last night, the first time I rewatched the footage of her, I couldn't take my eyes off it. I do need to reposition the little camera a little when I'm wearing it on the side because some of the time her face was out of the frame and I missed some of her expressions, which are so cute I never want to miss them ever again.

I want her to come up to my room and sit and talk. I want to make plans with her about what we're going to do.

Just knowing her makes me feel like I can go back to school. At least there would be a reason to be there. To pass her in the halls or maybe have a class with her.

She's the most interesting person I think I have ever met. I loved talking to her in the car and I loved talking to her after when I brought her home. I love all her different expressions and the way she talks.

I've never known anyone with such a direct yet hidden way of being.

I want to uncover all of it. If she has any secrets. I want her to tell them to me.

Like I tell her mine.

I want to know how she became the girl she is.

ALLY

think the thing I loved about her most, the thing I miss most now, is how funny she was. How daring. How she would make me do things I didn't think I could do. She was the one who wanted to go on the roller coaster. She was the one who insisted Daddy take us out on the boat that first time when we were still so small and she was not afraid to be out there.

When we were little she had such a funny way of getting me to do things. If I worried that she was climbing too high in the pine trees she would tell me to come up with her.

"C'mon, you be the prince and climb up my long hair," she'd say, hanging by her knees from a branch and letting her hair hang down. And once she got me to get into the low branches she always looked so happy and would make up stories about how we were explorers. Soon I'd be so drawn into what she was saying I wouldn't notice how high we were.

I remember one time we were so high—up in the narrow branches near the thin trunk at the top of a pine—and I could feel the treetop swaying beneath our weight. I started to get scared but Syd laughed. She couldn't have been happier that we were all the way up there. She couldn't have been more relaxed. If something was frightening, if it was hard, it was like she actually got more relaxed.

"It's not going to break!" she shouted to me. "It's going to bend with our weight. It's going to hold us." And she began swaying back and forth—we were up so high we could look down on other trees and on the top of our house and she had not a moment of fear that our feet would slip.

"Calm down," she said, and I did. I let myself sway in the treetop and look out at the blue sky and the rooftops and I didn't care about the sticky pine tar on my hands.

Those are the moments when I realize how much she gave me. If only I hadn't thought she was trying to push me away.

SYD

watched from the window as Ally stepped out of the Austin in Graham's driveway. There she was like a princess being brought home by *literally* "the boy next door." After the talk with Richards, this made me more sad than mad. But I was beginning to get mad anyway. I bet the main reason Ally decided she liked Graham is because he actually *is* the boy next door and that fits so well with her tiny-town-blueberry-picking-goody-goody way she decided she had to add him to the list of clichés that she lives by.

I would also be more angry at her if not for the fact that I had to protect her. It was weird the way Graham talked about Eric; he seemed to want Ally to be his new best friend, his new Eric, and he wanted me to take his drugs. She just wouldn't see that there was anything shady about Graham. Even if it was becoming plainer to other people. That this is one more way her trust in all people being good will get her into trouble. How on earth could she have had *me* for a sister for all these years and still think all people are good?

I slipped down the back stairs as Ally entered the house, and ran across the driveway into the bushes outside Graham's garage and watched him. He was standing by the car, looking kind of dazed with this grin on his face. His hair looked windblown and I could tell they had been making out. I was sure he had driven her out to the beach and she had told him stories about how our parents used to take us there when we were little or how our dad built all the beautiful old ships you see at the yacht club. I was sure she gave him our whole life story—her version of it.

The idea of her being so trusting to this weirdo, who moved from the south and who for some reason has been out of school under some questionable circumstances, circumstances that he'd maybe even been arrested for or his parents had been sued for, shocked even me. Ally had always been very selective about the boys she dated. The only thing I could think is that: A) this guy's looks had gone to her head, B) she had found some way to irritate me beyond telling on me when I smoked and complaining about my music, or C) Graham was a master at manipulating trusting girls. I decided it was probably all three and then walked around the hedge and into the garage. He was startled to see me.

"Stay away from my sister," I said.

"Whoa. *What?*"

"You heard me. I said, stay the fuck away from my

sister. Or you will pay for it."

His face fell. "Hey . . . uh . . . are you *okay?*"

"I'm fine. You're the one who's not going to be okay."

He took a step toward me. Touched my arm—and looked at me with his pale-blue eyes; pale, blue, screwed-up eyes—the pupils wide and black from all the shit he was taking. Some weird cocktail that made him hyper-focused, not afraid of anything, and never upset. I thought, That's just the kind of cocktail that's a recipe for disaster. And weed is illegal? Seriously? Something's not right in this world.

"Take it easy," he said. He ran his hand down my arm and then took my hand in his. I was about to pull away. I couldn't believe the nerve he had.

"You better—"

"Shhh," he said, putting one finger against my lips. I glared at him, but he pulled me closer to him. "I like you."

Then before I could say anything he leaned down and kissed me quickly on the mouth. I pushed him away and he just laughed. I stared at him, trying to figure out just why he thought he could get away with this. Who the hell did he think he was? I looked into his relaxed face and thought again about what Richards said about always being tough and I thought again that I'd like to try whatever he was on. Pills weren't my drug of choice but he was clearly having some kind of wonderful time just being himself.

"C'mon," Graham said. "Let me kiss you again. I really do like you. Even when you're like this."

Maybe I would let him kiss me again, I thought. Maybe that was the best way to find out who he really was and what he had going on. Maybe I liked it. And that's the hardest part to admit now. That maybe, in spite of everything my head told me, every creepy feeling I had about the whole situation, everything I knew about Ally falling in love with him . . . maybe, just maybe, I liked it.

I felt like that for maybe a week.

And then it all came crashing down.

SYD

eah," he said. "I don't think he's right either. I spent the whole day dragging him around the halls and he acted like . . . I don't know, some kind of smarmy spaced-out aristocrat. You know what I'm saying?"

"I do!" I told him. "I totally do! Becky and these girls at school seem to think he's some artist heartthrob Abercrombie model. Bitches be crazy."

"Yeah, well, the boy's hot," he said. "I'll give him that. But yeah. He's weird, and I don't mean weird like you."

"Hey!" I laughed and he put his arm around me. We were taking the back way home, meandering past the harbor and seeing the tall masts stately rocking in the distance. Walking out to the old pier, the one totally abandoned because the foundation was so badly eroded. The place was a briny brackish barnacle-covered part of the town that time forgot and I loved to walk there with

Declan—it was solitary and nostalgic and felt a little dangerous.

"He is hot," I said. "But not hot like you."

He gave my side a little squeeze. "Let's go to the old playground."

"Yeah. Let's do it," I said. We would go to the town hall playground and swing until nearly dusk and when everyone had gone home for dinner we would climb into the sprawling wooden jungle gym that looked like a castle. There were actually little rooms in there. And we would sit and get high and talk and do anything we wanted. After being interrupted by Ally, I was dying to touch him again. Feel his warm skin and his hard muscles.

We put our boards down and skated so we could get there faster.

Coasting from a distance we could see Graham's car parked across the street from the swing set.

As we approached the park, we could see him sitting there, wearing a red baseball cap, his messy blond hair hanging out beneath it. At first it looked like he was alone, but as we got closer we could see he was talking to a little kid—a boy maybe ten years old who was wearing an Iron Man T-shirt, a blue Windbreaker, and jeans.

"Sweet shirt that little dude has," Declan said. "I wonder where he got it."

"From his parents, duh. It's not like he can drive himself to the mall."

Declan laughed. "Does Graham have a little brother?" he asked.

"I don't think so," I said. "He strikes me as the ultimate only child."

"Takes one to know one," Declan said.

"What's that supposed to mean?" I asked.

"Just kidding, Tate. Wait. Hang on . . . shhh."

We picked up our boards and tiptoed quietly to the edge of the trees that flanked the swings and jungle gym. Graham hadn't noticed us and if the kid did he didn't think much of it.

We walked through the trees and stood silently listening.

"Oh yeah?" Graham was saying. "I had no idea. I always thought that Wolverine got bit by a wolf or something to get his powers."

Even from far away you could see the kid give him a little condescending smirk when he said it. The kid's voice was high-pitched and he talked some more while Graham nodded his head, listening.

"Spider-Man," Graham said. "You know, 'cause of the web shooting. He's pretty much a regular guy, lives with his aunt and all that. I think he's the best. When do you usually get out of school?"

The boy told him and Graham took out a little notebook. The same one he'd used when talking to Becky. At that point Declan and I looked at each other and slunk out from behind the trees.

"'Sup, G?" Declan asked him.

"Oh, hey guys." Graham seemed completely relaxed. "This is my friend Brian. He's a mutant with a metal-alloy skeleton who fights crime."

I was worried for one minute that Graham would act all weird because of what happened in his garage, but there was nothing strange between the two of us at all. He was focused completely on Brian.

The kid laughed and looked happy when Graham said it. He was obviously proud to be talking to a big kid and thrilled to have an audience for his information about the X-Men. I noticed that he was wearing a necklace. A cord with a piece of sea glass at the end of it. The letter *W* drawn on the glass with Sharpie marker. Becky's handiwork, of course. Pretty soon the whole town would be covered in sea glass jewelry and running on apps built by one adorable little stoner with a nose ring.

"Hey, Brian," we said.

He waved at us even though we were two feet away from him.

"Where's your mom?" I asked.

He turned and pointed to a bench at the far end of the playground where a woman was reading next to a stroller.

"What's up, kids?" Graham asked us, leaning back on the bench and folding his hands behind his head. "I suppose you have four hundred and twenty reasons you wanted to come to the park tonight?"

"Nah, we're just chillin'," Declan said.

"What are you up to?" I asked him.

"Making art," Graham said. And at that moment I noticed the tiny camera he was holding. The same one he had tried to film me with the other day. It was so small, I had again completely missed it. "Making art and talking to my homeboy Brian."

"What kind of art?" Declan asked.

"Cool stuff. If you want to come over I can show you."

Declan and I looked at each other. The playground castle would have to wait . . . or we'd have to sneak out later at night. Whatever Graham was working on, we needed to see it.

We said good-bye to Brian and got in Graham's car. Even though it was fall he had the top down. He drove fast through the winding shady roads that wound up the hill to our neighborhood. Declan sat in the front and I sat in the tiny backseat. Graham was a good driver. He took some of the hairpin turns a little fast, but it was fun and he definitely knew what he was doing. I imagined him driving all over country roads down south like some aristocratic hick, even though I knew he was from the suburbs.

When we parked in the driveway I saw Ally looking out our window at the three of us—but I ignored it and we quickly went inside.

It was one of those houses that was somehow even bigger on the inside. The whole place was painted white and had high ceilings and perfect track lighting like in an art gallery. And there were huge canvases hanging on the walls. I mean huge. Like taking up most of the room.

"That looks like it belongs in a museum," Declan said, pointing to a massive blue painting that looked like some kind of dangerous and mythological aquatic life.

Graham laughed. "It actually was in a museum for the past six months! Part of my stepmom's show at LACMA."

"What's LACMA?" I asked. "It sounds like a disease you get if you can't digest milk."

"Los Angeles County Museum of Art." Graham laughed. "Next week Kim will be sending it to a museum in Florence."

And it was suddenly very easy to imagine all the boys at school who liked to hunt and fish and fix boats kicking Graham's ass in the school parking lot. Maybe he knew this too and it was why he didn't go to school.

The rest of the house was equally beautiful and weird. I guess Kim also decorated everything. Because things looked expensive and hard to find. A chandelier made from deer antlers hung above a long rectangular table in the dining room. The couch was upholstered in some kind of beautiful fabric that looked like trees and fire.

"The couch fabric looks like a forest fire," Declan said.

"It is. It's a screen print of the fires outside Oakland a few years ago."

I couldn't decide if this kid's parents were a nightmare or

the coolest parents in town. There was a large photograph of things I could barely identify; it looked like silk fabric and knives and horses' hooves all mixed together. Graham saw me looking at it and pointed to the signature in the corner.

"That's an original Kate Steciw," he said. "It's worth half a million dollars. C'mon, let's take the back stairs." We followed him through the long hallway to the back of the house where floor-to-ceiling windows looked out on the woods and a yard that had a tall marble fountain in it. But it was not like a garden fountain, something that shot water or had stones or figures in it. It was shaped like a drinking fountain. A rectangular block of marble that was a complete replica with a little stream of water arcing and falling. You could imagine some giant leaning over to get a drink. It was a visual joke. A play on the idea of fountains.

"Let me guess," I said, gesturing to it. "Kim."

Graham nodded and laughed and then sprinted up the wide oak staircase, taking two steps at a time. We followed him until we reached the third floor of his house—the attic, I guess—but finished better than any attic I'd ever seen. We have the widow's walk, which is cool, because you can see the whole harbor from there, but it's a cold and desolate place to hang out. Here dark curtains hung down from the ceiling and there was a small row of seats like in a real movie theater facing a blank white wall.

"This is the screening room," he said.

"Wow," said Declan, "where did you get the movie theater seats?"

"At an architectural salvage warehouse," Graham told us. "Have a seat."

We watched him fiddle around with some kind of digital projector and then he turned off the lights and sat next to us. He was very excited and I could feel the kind of pent-up exuberant energy coming off him. He sat down between us, and his arm touched my arm. I could feel the warmth of his skin and I let my finger brush his wrist for a moment. It gave me goose bumps to touch him and to know he wanted me to touch him. He was shaking slightly, excited about showing us the movie, or nervous that I was there with Declan. The way his body seemed so receptive to everything beside me in the dark, it felt like he was on some kind of speed or maybe even Ecstasy. I pulled myself together and leaned the other way to feel my shoulder touching the solid shoulder of Declan. Then I took his hand.

Suddenly the wall in front of us was flooded with white light beaming from the projector. And then the images started. Stark and brilliantly full of color. There was a close-up of Becky's lips while she was talking but no audio and the footage was slowed down. Smoke came out of her mouth and then the footage was reversed and it looked like she was sucking in a big cloud of gray smoke. Then there were shots of girls jumping rope and chasing each other but they looked like they were taken from old movies. Then footage of a cat eating a mouse. A slow cruising shot of the whole neighborhood, the cheerleading squad practicing but shot from far away and it looked like from the top of a building or something. Then Becky's lips again. Smiling, talking. We could clearly read her lips and she was saying, "Yeah, you should text me . . ." Declan nudged me.

Next shot was the inside of a medicine cabinet with rows of prescription bottles set up, waves crashing and rolling in and then the same footage backward. All of the sound was mismatched—the sound of the waves accompanied Becky smoking, and the sound of the girls playing went with the cruising shots of the neighborhood. The cheerleading squad had the sound of some kid talking about outer space while they did their drills. Then suddenly on the screen there was Allyson walking up the driveway with her backpack, going inside our house and shutting the door. It was also shot from above—and looked like it was directly above her head somehow. The last frame was of that kid Brian at the park—apparently today wasn't the first time Graham had talked to him. He was holding a Wolverine action figure and making it jump around. There was an extreme close-up on the kid's face, his big blue eyes and smile, and then he turned his head quickly as if he heard something—like he was startled and a little worried. Then there was Allyson again—sitting in Graham's backyard looking up at him from the grass.

Graham stood up suddenly and stopped the projector.

"You get the idea," he said. "There's another hour of this or so . . . other random stuff." He seemed a little flustered and I couldn't tell if it was because he didn't want us to see the footage of Ally, or because he felt weird that I was there with Declan, or maybe just his drugs were wearing off.

He turned the lights back on and we sat in the weird mini theater not saying anything. I'm sure Declan was thinking what I was thinking, which was that this kid was from another planet.

"It's pretty good, man," Declan said. "Pretty good. You really know how to use that camera. I don't know how you got some of those shots. Wow. I mean, that's . . . What the hell is it about?"

Graham shrugged. "It's about—"

"No, wait! Wait!" Declan yelled, doing his typical Declan-nerd-boy thing where he thinks he's figured every- thing out and wants to shout it out before anyone else can. He's been doing this since third grade. "I know! I know, it's about how everyone is in and of themselves a spectacle. Am I right? How every individual act is also kind of a performed act? That's it! That's it! Am I right? Except for Tate walking into her house. Right? Or maybe even that! Wow! That is awesome, actually."

Graham looked disappointed. "Um, it's kind of almost the opposite. It's about how people are not quite real until they are observed or filmed. You know, like if a tree falls in the woods and no one's there, does it make a sound?"

Declan said, "Huh. Sure . . . but—"

"I'm sorry," I said. "It looks really, really cool, but what does any of that even freaking mean? Of course people are real."

Graham looked disappointed for a minute and then regained his usual hip, I-got-a-secret face and leaned back in his chair. "So you think all people are real?" he asked me, looking right into my eyes. "Aren't there some people who aren't?"

It scared me—really scared me for a second. "No," I said. "Of course not."

"Wait wait wait!" Declan interrupted us. "This is really interesting. So you're filming people to make them real?"

"That's right," Graham said.

"Huh," Declan said. "Okay, okay, I get where you might be coming from. As a history buff, you really believe that identity is reified by its documentation."

"*What?*" Graham said, sounding genuinely confused and annoyed. "Speak English."

"Have you shown these to anyone else?" I asked before Declan could go off on some weird tangent about who makes history and what it means. I could hear that one coming a mile away and already I was tired of being trapped between these two nerds.

Graham got a faraway look on his face. "Yeah," he said quietly. "Lots and lots of people have seen my films." Then he started to look genuinely sad. "Some of them have sold for five thousand dollars. And I think the people who buy them even know what they mean," he said. "These movies make their life better." He looked like he might start crying. "They get me," he said. "They understand."

POLICE CHIEF BILL WERTZ

We didn't believe it at first. It looked like a normal Tumblr page. You opened it up and there were links to click on to watch his films. Harmless stuff for the most part. A little full of himself, but what seventeen-year-old boy isn't?

When we looked closer we realized he had a hidden site—something that only members could access. The whole thing was under the name Copeland Productions—not a very sophisticated secret name. And the Amazon wish list was also under that name. And that list was long and extravagant. I'd say he's been bought tens of thousands of dollars in merchandise by his "fans" in exchange for these films.

And the films. I can barely describe them to you . . . It makes me want to . . . It makes you sick to think that this is the world we live in. That all this was going on in this beautiful tree-lined neighborhood among these decent people.

SYD

Once we got out of Prince Charming's weirdo castle, we walked back into the woods.

"That kid is not too bright," Declan said. "I think he's kinda dumb, actually, which I didn't quite realize when I was showing him around school. But he's come to some erroneous ideas about how the world works."

"That's all you have to say?"

"Oh well. He clearly knows how to frame a shot, I mean, that's undeniable, he's talented, but—"

"No! I mean you just think he's *dumb*? That's it?"

Declan nodded. "Yeah. Dumb and really materialistic," he said. "It's that simple."

"I guess you're right," I said. "I guess I always think people like that are kinda dangerous."

"Nah," Declan said, shaking his head. "They're mostly harmless, just annoying. At first I thought this guy was real trouble too. But he's just some geeked-out kid making art who doesn't have the brains yet to know what it means or why he's doing it. Maybe he really will be famous someday."

"What about that thing he said about people buying his movies?" I asked.

"*That?* That, my dear young lady, is a thing some boys do called bragging. I'm pretty sure it is an enormous exaggeration."

"C'mon," I said, grabbing his hand and pulling him farther into the woods. "We already missed dinner, let's go for a walk so people can have a chance to worry about where we are." I said it even though it would only be his parents and maybe Ally worrying about where we were.

He laughed and followed me though the pines out into a little clearing. The ground was soft with hundreds of years of decayed pine needles and it smelled amazing. It was already beginning to grow dark when we reached the giant moss-covered stone and climbed on top of it. Declan sat and I stood, leaning my head back to look up at the beautiful canopy of branches, the blazing orange light of late afternoon cutting through the dark branches and creating a strobe effect. He held my legs steady while I arched my back and gazed skyward and then he pulled me down to sit on his lap.

We smoked and held hands, and I said, "I can't wait until we get out of this town."

"Yeah, baby," Declan said. "Just a couple more years,

we're going to freaking Stanford."

"Or Harvard."

"Or straight to hell," he said, grinning.

I kissed him and he put his hands in my hair. I felt like I was melting into him. I rubbed my hand over the front of his jeans and could feel him getting excited. It always seemed like Declan's mind was racing but when we were making out, it was just the two of us. So amazing. Like time actually stopped and there was nothing else to do in the whole world but suck on Declan's lips.

"If no one sees us doing this, is it really happening?" I joked.

He laughed. And I am sure we were both thinking about what an upside-down world Graham lived in, where you exist only when there's some photographic evidence of you.

Before we realized it—it was dark. We walked back through the woods to the edge of my driveway—the property line between Graham's house and mine. And we stood behind my house kissing. He pressed me up against the side of the garage and slipped his hand up my shirt and inside my bra. I looked back at the house and saw the light of the kitchen window.

Allyson was standing there. She was looking out into the woods. Just staring blankly into nothing. Sometimes I think when I'm not around or when Mom is not telling her what to do, she just shuts down. I had no idea if she had ever leaned against the garage and felt a boy's hard body pressing into her. But I knew she was missing a lot. And maybe dull-witted handsome Graham was the boy who would make her want to finally do more than homework and bake blueberry muffins.

I gave Declan a last tight squeeze and he put his skateboard down on the driveway.

"Tomorrow, Miss Tate?"

"You bring the herb and I'll bring the flame."

He high-fived me and skated away and I watched him cruise down the driveway and out onto the cool autumn street. The tall ornate streetlamps started to turn on one by one as he passed beneath them and I thought what a badass Declan Wells was. And how lucky I was to know him.

GRAHAM

4:21—Tate going into her house
4:34—Tate in her bedroom
5:00—Playground outside after-school program
6:00—Tate kneeling in front of Declan in the woods

Dear Lined Piece of Paper,

I get the feeling people here think I'm weird. I'm trying to do what Dr. Adams says and focus and stay interested in what they are doing. Ask them questions about their lives. But mostly what I want to do is watch movies. You would think there would be plenty of kids at this school who would be down with such a simple thing like that. But no. The pretty Tate girl is still on my mind constantly. I invited her over but I don't think she understood what it is I'm trying to do.

I'm starting to make money on the films. I've decided to call it an encyclopedia or a directory. A person can buy an individual entry or the whole directory. The individual entry is five thou-sand dollars. The whole encyclopedia is fifty thousand dollars. I could make an insane amount of money in a very short time. Enough to finance my long film. Enough to do it all by myself.

I feel like she alone could understand if she would just let herself—if she would be with me alone and let me talk to her. I feel like the two of us could make movies that would change the way everyone thought. The kind of movie I made back in Vir-ginia with Eric.

Dr. Adams is still trying to get me to talk about Eric. Maybe if I could make another movie like the one I made with him I could just show it to Dr. Adams. I could say, Here. Do you get it now? Do you understand? Because Eric got it! Eric fucking understood. Eric knew exactly how I felt. He'd had the same prescription as me since he was like eight years old. If we had a sleepover and someone forgot the Ritalin—no problem, there was plenty to go around. And when we got older we figured out how to mix things just right. Eric and I were so close we were barely different people.

Dr. Adams looks interested and concerned when I say things like this but I know Tate will understand completely. I know she will. And I know we are going to be together forever. When I film her, I can feel how real she is. How solid and grounded and real. If anyone knows this world is bullshit and the way around it is to do your own thing, if anyone understands—has ever understood—it's her.

SYD

I knew the thing I had to do was find out what happened between Graham and Ally. She had been keeping things from me, there was no doubt. Acting all weird like there was something she was trying to tell me, but I had been so pissed at her she couldn't find the courage to do it.

I'd already threatened Graham and I was afraid if I tried to talk to him again, I'd end up rolling around on the floor with him in his room or having to watch some other film that looked like spliced-up surveillance footage from a convenience-store camera and then have to listen to him say that's what he intended it to look like.

The thing is this. If you pay attention, if you watch the news or pay attention in any way, you know that little towns like ours are always hiding some nut or other. In the case of Graham, I couldn't tell what he was up to. He filmed Becky. He filmed our neighbors. He filmed himself.

Christ, he filmed that little Brian kid talking about freaking X-Men for like an hour. That's when I knew it was not just artistic inspiration but also something else. Maybe the drugs. Who in the hell can listen to a ten-year-old talk about superheroes with such concentration and attention to detail unless they are using a little Adderall?

I started to worry that he had gotten Allyson to do something she didn't want to. Or he had footage of us that he'd taken from across the driveway.

I knew I had to get into his house to find out what was going on.

And I would have done it sooner if the whole town hadn't been swept up in a crisis.

And what happened next was so strange. So unexpected it was even more confusing about who Graham Copeland really was.

I knew the answers were all somewhere in his room. But I never expected what I would find there.

ALLY

had been thinking about him nonstop since the ride in his Austin and the long talk we had about his friends and how life was back in Virginia. I was distracted at school. I baked him two batches of muffins. And then finally I asked him to come out on the boat with me and my parents. Of course, Syd would not go. She hated sailing. She used to love it when we were kids but now she had some big grudge against it, like it was stupid or wrong or something our parents did to ignore us.

They didn't sail to ignore us. The harbor and building was Daddy's life and if we wanted to be a part of his life, we had to do the things he wanted to do. I don't know why this was so hard for Syd to understand, but I didn't really care that much either. It kept her out of our hair and let me have a lot of time with Graham, and it was nice for him to meet our parents without Syd showing up and saying some wise-ass thing or talking about Declan nonstop.

As usual, Daddy didn't say much. He shook Graham's hand roughly and gave him a little thump on the back. He said, "Can you sail, then?"

When Graham said no, Daddy shook his head a little and shifted his pipe to the other side of his mouth, then went to rig up the sails. But Mom stood next to him and asked him questions.

She asked him if he'd like a drink and then went below into the hold and made us club sodas and lime, which she put in two plastic martini glasses. She made herself a real martini and then began asking Graham if he was related to certain people she knew in Virginia. Mom was always so charming. I loved the way she talked to people. I think she was probably the best hostess in all of Rockland, maybe in the whole state.

Dad pulled up the anchor and we headed out and I saw the look of joy and fascination on Graham's face as we tacked out into the middle of the harbor and then the wind picked up and pushed us along.

Mommy and I were wearing matching outfits and Daddy sat gazing out at the ocean, manning the rudder and shouting to me to handle the rigging. "Ready about! Hard-a-lee. Dammit, gal, I said hard to the leeward side—we don't want to lose our wind."

I showed Graham how to do it and he looked so happy it was amazing. He had his camera with him, of course. He'd attached it to the brim of his hat and I'm sure it was capturing some beautiful footage of the sea.

Once we were cruising along for some time Graham and I sat on the bow together and felt wind and talked.

"You're incredible," he said. "I've never met anyone like you. Never met a family like yours."

I couldn't believe he was talking to me this way. I'm a very simple person and I know it. But he acted like I was something so complex. Like I was special.

"No one has more secret skills than you," he said. "You're full of surprises every time I turn around."

To: harlanadams@mind2mindpsychotherapy.com
From: david.copeland@copelandconsulting.com

Dear Dr. Adams,

The new regimen seems to be working well for Graham. He's been more focused and self-assured and seems to have developed a bit of a social life. Kim says he's been having some friends over and watching movies. We're beginning to feel that he might be able to transition into some healthy way of using media in his life.

Kim is still convinced that he has a future as a filmmaker and it would be cruel to limit his use of the screening room or constantly monitor his activities. She's found a very good way to keep track of what he is doing by setting up "studio visits." These are things that real artists do to have their work critiqued. She regularly watches all the movies he's made as part of these studio visits and I think it's giving Graham a sense of creative purpose and allows us to keep track of his activities without seeming like we are spying on him.

I didn't believe it could happen but I am feeling more confident than ever that he will be able to live a full life after the trauma.

He's also started talking about Eric again. I don't know if this is the result of something you are doing in therapy or if the creative work is making him take stock of his life and making him remember the bond the boys had.

He's mentioned several times things that they used to do together, and he regularly expresses pride in how tough and smart Eric was. Yesterday he said he would give anything to just have something of Eric's. It nearly broke my heart. If it wasn't for the bad blood I would almost feel inclined to contact Eric's family to see if that was possible. But I am sure once the settlement payment cleared they were happy to never hear from us again. Such a pity. We all ache for their loss. And no one feels it more profoundly than Graham.

Lately I get the sense that he is finally capable of expressing himself and maybe looking for another friend who he can bond with. These days that possibility seems most likely from the next-door neighbors.

They even invited Graham to go out on an early fall excursion on their boat. I don't think I've ever seen him as happy as when he returned home, his cheeks red and hair windblown. He looked like he'd had some great epiphany. Raced up to his room, he said to take some notes. This move may be the best decision we ever made. The ocean is certainly an inspiration and maybe just the kind of combination of adventure and wholesome activity that can reach him.

Looking forward to meeting with you to discuss his progress this coming Wednesday.

Take care, Doc, and thank you.

GRAHAM

1:34—*Cleaning the decks*
4:01—*Tate tying knots close up*
7:55—*Coastline, lowering boom*
15:03—*Below deck*
20:00–65:04—*Talking with Julia*

Dear Lined Piece of Paper,
She wasn't kidding about being able to sail with her father!
That girl is so at home on the ocean she's like some superhero. I
think I'll tell Brian there's a new superhero named Tate who
battles sharks. That kid believes pretty much anything anyone
tells him.

Mr. Tate is awesome. He actually smokes a pipe! I think he
had it in the corner of his mouth the entire time we were out in
the harbor. He doesn't talk much at all—more like grunts and
points to things. Mrs. Tate is like some kind of celebrity. They

both have funny accents, but very different from each other's. Mr. Tate actually built the ship himself and apparently li'l miss Tate used to go out on it with him when she was just a toddler.

That girl is amazing.

Her mother was not much of a sailor but she was very funny. She reminded me of the people who buy Kim's paintings. And she was dressed in some kind of perfect sailing suit. She and Tate dressed alike. White shorts and blue-and-white-striped T-shirts and red sweaters with a picture of an anchor on them and Docksiders. It was really funny and kinda cool to film.

Sooo. Dr. Adams changed the drugs. Dad and Kim think he's some kind of genius. But really the thing that is making me so happy is that I doubled the dose. Obviously. Whatever he changed it to did not take into account I had already changed the dosages of the other stuff like six months ago. I can buy all of it online— well, I don't buy it myself; it's on my private wish list, which I send out to people who buy more than one hundred dollars of my films. They pay and the stuff comes in boxes that look like books or prints. Dr. Adams started asking me about dosages and I figured eventually they'd figure things out—so this method works best because it doesn't worry anyone. Anyway . . . all this is to say I guess this new doubling the dose is more like quadrupling it.

How can someone who is not me know how I feel just by things I've told him? It doesn't make any sense. I know how I feel on this stuff and I know the kind of state I need to maintain to produce good work and I am not going to let that stop. Also—if they stop prescribing it I can just get shit online. He took me off the Xanax because he said I seem to have the anxiety under control. That's because I already got myself some Librium and have been taking it for weeks! The Librium combined with Effexor, and the Adderall from Dr. Adams, is pretty sweet. Add to that the occasional half bottle of NyQuil to give things that floating sparkling effect that makes things beautiful and you're good to go. But overall I am focused, relaxed, and ready to achieve greatness.

The kind of greatness Eric always talked about. After sailing with Tate, I started to feel like Rockland might have been one of the more beautiful places I had ever been and I started to think that maybe I could make enough films and sell them and not actually have to go to school at all. I would wander around looking for good subjects.

It's amazing how much money people pay just for a simple little interview with a child. Near the skate park, near the elementary school, there's always interesting subjects. For example, Julia Blair, who I talked to. She was playing on the swings and then she jumped off and was sitting by herself near the sandbox, clearly waiting for someone to pick her up. She was wearing a pink shirt and a little dark-green cardigan sweater with pictures of tulips on it. I sat on the swings. I had my camera attached to my hat as usual. And I was pretty sure I was getting some beautiful footage. The woods behind her—the contrasting colors of her clothes, the way she played absently by herself, looked distracted and thoughtful. I knew this would look good edited together with footage of things I had taken off the news or footage of cars driving really fast.

Finally I asked her, *"Are you waiting for someone to pick you up?"*

She nodded. *"I'm waiting for my babysitter. She should be here soon."*

"You don't walk home by yourself? You seem like a big girl."

"I do on Wednesday and Friday, but today my babysitter's taking me to her house. I'm in third grade. My mom says I can stay at home by myself soon."

She told me she lives on Westmont. While she was talking I was thinking how cool it would be to get little kids to describe the whole geography of the city. How it would be really weird. And I could intercut the descriptions with footage of highways and maybe old pictures of Rockland. I was sure the same people who usually buy my films would pay even more if I had a film with lots of kids talking about their neighborhoods and how they walked around, how they saw it. Maybe I could even get a production company interested in it.

"Do you have any friends who might want to be in a movie?" I asked her.

"Maybe," she said. *"But can I be a princess in it?"*

I told her of course. It really didn't matter what she was going to be. People would buy the movie no matter what.

I lay down on the grass near her and pointed the camera up at the sky—the canopy of trees overhead and the blue and the clouds. And it felt like the world was full of possibility. I left before her babysitter came to pick her up and went out to drive the Austin Healey on the beautiful winding roads of Rockland.

POLICE CHIEF BILL WERTZ

Apparently it was on some kind of automatic system. Once people had paid enough to his PayPal account or bought him everything from his Amazon wish list, the video would automatically download from his site. There were already dozens of films. I thought the worst were the ones of kids. Talking to them about what they liked and then asking them questions about where they lived and went to school and who picked them up and when. The films were basically doing all the groundwork for any pedophile who wanted to come along. I couldn't believe them when I saw them. He was literally assisting the potential abduction—the potential harm—to a child.

One little girl gave her address, phone number, school, and listed all the streets she walked home on and what time. Our jaws dropped when we saw it.

According to his parents, that was some kind of point he

was making with his art. Like the films were a comment on what he was actually doing. That they were about trust and how the world has changed and how we are all constantly being watched and have no privacy and are at risk for people harming us . . . and God knows what other excuses these people came up with for what he was doing. They were blind to what their kid was up to. This was not art. This was some kid with a camera seeing how far he could push it, how much he could get away with. How he could get any attention at all. This is a very sick, very spoiled kid and nothing more. In the end, when I look back on it it's amazing only two people were killed. The potential harm was so great.

And who knows if some new terror will come out of it.

ALLY

probably did it to spite her, I can see that now. Syd told me to stay away from Graham and then she and Declan went over there. Watched movies with him. She literally did that the day after she told me not to hang out with him. I knew that he was just another boy she would treat badly. I'd seen her do it before. I wanted to be friends with him and I wanted to do something interesting in my life before I went off to college. Something daring. I wanted to be with someone who could appreciate me for who I was and also show me things I didn't know about. Syd is so crazy the way she exaggerates. "Stay away from him or it'll ruin everything we have," she said. I mean, please. I was like, "What exactly do we have? We haven't had one good conversation since we were ten years old."

Syd never introduced me to her friends. We used to play with Becky together when we were little but Declan—I don't think he's even said a word to me. The two of them are always off together. If I come in the room and they are there, she pretends I'm not there and says "Let's go" to him and he makes kind of an awkward face and then does whatever she wants. I started thinking about all the things Sydney had excluded me from. How after elementary school she pretty much ignored me at all times. And when she started smoking dope, and doing God knows what else she and her stoner friends get up to, it's like I don't even exist.

Graham was maybe the first person who hung out with us together a lot because he lived next door. And because of the way we met—all of us standing out there by the edge of the woods. We would sometimes hang out talking together. He seemed to really like both of us and be interested in both of us. He was weird and cool and had something rebellious in him like Syd and he cared about things the way I did. At first, I thought he was maybe one of those academic stars that she always liked to be around and then I realized he was gentler and shier. More like me.

Anyway I had all this on my mind and also the whole thing about going off to college. I used to look at it as a great adventure, but the closer I got to leaving the more I thought of it as being gotten rid of, maybe permanently. I know our parents loved me and that it wasn't true but I felt like Sydney had outgrown everything about me and wanted me gone. I wanted to get away from her too. I did. But I couldn't help feeling like I was the one who was being cast out and might never be a part of her life again. Even her talking about us coming together and being unified about things also freaked me out. For some reason it made me feel more like she was getting rid of me—not less. It was so unlike her. I just felt in those days like I was about to disappear.

So I did it. I did. I went over to his house because he invited me. And went up to his room. The house was amazing. Though it looked smaller than I thought it would be after seeing it from the outside. There were these tiny little paintings hanging all over. A whole wall taken up with miniatures that looked like they had been painted with a single eyelash they were so delicate. The house was really tastefully done. Not in the cozy New England style my mother preferred, but in a sophisticated way. Outside in the backyard there was a marble fountain with a single long smooth stone in the middle—it looked like one of those polished stone sculptures we studied in art history. I think the artist was Brancusi.

And I went up to his room. It was incredibly neat. Completely organized. It was more like a suite in a fancy hotel. He had his own bathroom connected to the room and the furniture was all really nice. He had a big old oak four-poster bed. The room was bright and on a corner with windows that overlooked the woods and also our house. His room was right across from our room. It was cool and quiet and he had shelves of interesting artifacts—things he said his parents and grandparents had brought back from traveling, or things people bought him as payment for the movies he made. He had more stuff than anyone I'd ever met. A massive record collection—I mean an actual vinyl record collection—that took up one wall of the room, another set of shelves from ceiling to floor lined with books, and another wall of electronic equipment—film stuff I guess. And then he had a closet full of stuff—some of it still in packages. Different kinds of cameras and lights and cables and microphones.

He also had an extremely thin flat-screen TV and that I guess is what we were going to watch his movies on—or that's what he asked me over to do anyway: watch movies.

He hooked up his camera and I sat in a big comfortable leather chair in the corner by the windows and then he set up a tripod. He stood behind it looking at me and looking down at the camera every once in a while.

"Is this okay?" he asked.

I shrugged. "Sure. I guess."

"You're really beautiful," he said, and I covered my face, embarrassed.

"Okay," he said. "What's your name?"

"Allyson Tate."

He looked confused for just a second and then smiled.

"Where do you live?"

"Next door to you."

"You're the girl next door." He smiled and looked up at me as he said it.

I could feel myself blushing. "I am," I said.

"Where do you go to school?" He adjusted some things on the camera. Messed with the focus or the light or something.

"RHS," I said.

"What kinds of things do you like to do?"

I shrugged. "I like baking." It made me smile to think about. "I like riding my bike. I like going out in the boat with my dad . . . gardening."

He was looking very intently at me. Studying me, but also smiling. Boys have looked at me, of course they have, but I don't think any boy had ever looked at me like that. Certainly not a boy as handsome as Graham Copeland.

"Where do you work?" he asked.

"Pine Grove Inn."

"What are your hours?"

"You know . . . after school until nine on Wednesday and Thursday and then Saturday mornings. I also just come when they need me."

"You're a fascinating creature, Allyson Tate," he said, and I shook my head. Even I knew that wasn't true. I was a capable Mainer. I loved my parents and my little town and I would probably end up buying a house like my parents had and fixing it up and going sailing with my own kids when I grew up. I knew I wasn't fascinating, that I probably looked like some girl from an L.L.Bean catalog. But maybe being happy with all the traditional things is what made me interesting to him. Maybe being able to find blueberry patches, to make a good "lobstah dinnah," to winterize an old house, or to love your parents—maybe those were some rare qualities I'd overlooked in myself.

He came around from behind the camera and sat next to me. And we both looked awkwardly at the lens for a while.

"I have one more question," he said.

I could feel the hair on the back of my neck stand up. Because I thought I knew what he was going to ask. "Okay," I said.

"Can I kiss you?"

I took a sharp breath and then laughed. "But . . . with the . . ." I pointed at the camera.

"Yeah." He nodded. "I mean, *no* if you don't want to. Of course, if you don't want to, but, uh . . . well . . . I just want to kiss you on camera so I can feel like I kissed a movie star. I don't think I'll believe it myself if I don't have evidence. We can record over it. I just. I . . . ah. Never mind."

I shook my head at him and laughed, and for a minute I didn't even remember he was filming us at all. I didn't care.

I could smell his hair, which was clean and smelled a little like cinnamon.

"I . . . um . . . sure," I said. "Sure. Yes." And I could feel my heart racing and I laughed again, not even knowing that I was going to.

And then he held my face in his hands and he kissed me. And then he kissed me again. And again. And again.

KIM

felt so validated by the move to Maine. Things were going as planned. Graham was thriving. Simply thriving. He would have an amazing portfolio to send off to wherever he decided. And he seemed to have boundless energy. He wasn't the shy, broken boy we arrived with. It was so gratifying for me to see him turning into a real artist. Someone who put the art before everything else. And just as I suspected that made him blossom, open up, start talking and thinking about things we were afraid he'd simply buried.

I think the best way to describe this brief period of his life is as a kind of creative atonement. It was astonishing how much he could do with the simple tools he had.

That second month in Maine was one of the best in our lives. David had cut back on his work and was around more. Helping Graham with his car. We ate dinner together every evening and screened films up in the attic room. Graham and I looked at each other's work and gave each other comments and critiques. The first month was bumpy, but the second seemed magical. I could see how David and I were going to be when we were old and traveling to different countries to see the amazing art of our amazing son. I imagined it many times. But now those thoughts are just a memory. The last memory of happiness we have.

BECKY

It was a big mistake to hit the pipe before I went down to breakfast. My mom was acting all weird and I couldn't tell if it was because she was actually acting all weird or because I was high. She looked totally freaked-out, and at first I thought maybe she knew I was high or she found my stash or something. Or maybe it was the way I was dressed. I was all in black, but I had a fishing-line necklace I made out of sea glass and broken-up circuit boards that I thought was probably the coolest thing I'd ever made in my life, and generally my mom disapproved of me smashing up my electronics stuff and turning it into jewelry. She could be pretty conservative in her tastes, and I was waiting for a comment—then I realized there was something big going on. Something bad in the news.

I said, "What's wrong?" and she just handed me the paper—she looked like she had been crying a little. I took it and looked at the headline: AMBER ALERT FOR ROCKLAND BOY, and a picture of this cute little chub in a baseball cap. I looked again and realized it was Brian Phillips—our cleaning lady's son. He'd been over to the house plenty of times and was really sweet. I loved Brian Phillips! I even showed him how to write some code one day after school. My hands started shaking. I wished I wasn't high. I felt sick.

"Oh my God!" I shouted. "This is terrible!"

My mother nodded and then she came over and put her arms around me. Hugged me tight I guess partly to reassure herself. "Jenny Phillips must be out of her mind with worry," she said, still holding me.

"I can't imagine," I said, hugging her back. I put my head on her shoulder. The news was the biggest, most terrible buzzkill ever, and I barely felt high anymore, just really upset.

The story in the paper said that the last time Brian was seen was by his friends just before he took the turn off to the street where he lived. That was after school yesterday at about 3:10. Around 3:40 his mother started calling his friends, and then at 4:30 she called the police. Someone must have taken him between his house and the corner.

Unfortunately there were no witnesses.

My mom started crying. "We should have paid her more," she said suddenly. "She would have been able to get him a phone if she had more money, or be there to pick him up herself if she didn't have to work so hard. Why didn't we pay her more? We could afford it. Oh, poor Jenny." Then I hugged her while she cried on my shoulder. "Poor little Brian," she kept saying. "Poor little guy."

I said, "It's not your fault, Mom. It's going to be okay. They'll find him." She nodded and apologized for crying and then started crying again.

I didn't feel like eating. I just had a glass of orange juice and then headed off to school.

"Be careful, Becky," my mom said. "Please. Just call me when you get to school today, Okay? Just this once."

"I will, Mom," I said. "Don't worry, someone will find him." I left her sitting, stunned, in front of the television. Listening for any updates about the AMBER Alert.

I got outside and could see what the news had already done. I don't think there was one kid or even a group of kids walking without someone's mom or dad right there with them. It was like the whole town had become tense and paranoid overnight. Brian was a really nice little kid. He was the kind of kid who just talked to everyone, super friendly and chatty and kinda never stopped talking. Lots of people knew him because of that, which I thought was a good thing. It seemed likely someone would recognize him—and I thought he'd be more likely to find a way to get help, to talk to someone.

I walked up Euclid Avenue and stopped at the corner to light a cigarette and to wait for Tate and Declan so we could walk the rest of the way to school. I figured they would have heard the news, but I could tell even watching them walk from a distance that they hadn't. They were laughing and bumping shoulders as they walked.

When they got close enough to see my face, Tate said, "Whoa, what's up, Becks?"

"Brian Phillips was kidnapped," I said.

"Who?"

"Little Brian! Jenny Phillips's kid? Our cleaning lady's kid. Don't you know him? He's a cute chubby little motor-mouth, talks about X-Men?"

At that they looked at each other and their eyes went wide.

"Oh my God!" Tate said, turning pale.

"We just saw him last week," Declan said, trying to sound calm. "Talking to Graham."

ALLY

started getting rides home with him every day after school. Syd was usually in detention so she wasn't there to hassle me. He'd pick me up in the Austin and we'd drive home along the harbor looking at the ocean, sometimes stop at the beach. Sometimes we'd get out and walk along and collect stones. And he always brought his camera. He'd ask me questions or film the ocean rolling in. I got used to being with him and to being on film and to the quiet times we had.

He did take drugs for his ADHD and for the stuff he had gone through. I didn't pressure him to tell me what had happened back in Virginia. But he told me most of it and I knew those were things I should keep to myself. He'd been hurt enough without everyone in Rockland finding out what happened. I knew he had different conversations with Syd than he had with me and I didn't care. I knew she was interested in the drugs he was taking and the problems he'd had but I was interested in how things could be better for him. I believed in him and I believed in his art. And I liked being independent of Syd. I liked what knowing him was doing to me. How it was changing me.

We were at the pier and the ocean breeze was blowing my hair and my skirt. The salt air and ocean smell at once familiar and exotic. Graham put his arm around me and pulled me closer to him to keep me warm and we listened to the waves and to the stones clacking together as the sea washed over them

"I had a dream about you last night," he said. "I had a dream we were out in the Austin driving along these winding roads and I was filming you and your hair was whipping around in the wind and you were laughing. You were standing up on the seat with your arms stretched out. It was like you could fly."

I nestled my head against his chest as we walked. "What else happened?"

I didn't look up but could feel him smiling beside me. That way he had where he would go quiet and just grin. He was always some strange combination of shy and confident, I couldn't quite explain.

"You said you wanted to go visit Eric, to meet Eric."

I nodded. "I do want to visit Eric," I said. "He sounds really cool."

"Maybe," he said. "Maybe we can. And then in the dream I pulled you back down into the seat and then suddenly we were out in this field of red flowers by this bridge and there was fog and smoke everywhere and we were kissing and . . . you know, we were, uh . . . it was . . ."

I knew what he meant. I'd had dreams like this about him too. I would never think to tell him about them though and I felt like he was really brave to bring it up, to even be able to talk like this.

"Did you have a girlfriend back in Virginia?" I asked.

He shook his head. "No. I mean, I had crushes on people, but really I spent all my time with Eric. I didn't take things very seriously, I guess. I didn't know how to ask a girl out. What about you? Did you ever have a boyfriend?"

I said, "Nobody all that important, I guess."

"What about Declan?"

"*What?*" I asked. "*Declan?*" This was just weird. I mean I know he saw Declan probably coming and going from our house all the time but clearly he had to know who he was visiting.

"Declan is Syd's friend," I said.

Graham looked really uncomfortable to have even brought it up.

"I think he's more than her friend," he said. "Uh . . . so . . . *you've* never been interested in him?"

He started to sound a little jealous and I really couldn't figure out why.

I said, "Declan? No. Of course not. I wouldn't even think of it."

SYD

BECKY

Uh, hello? Can you tell me why we are sitting in the Laundromat?"

"Shh. Don't be fucking stupid. I'm trying to think. And can you come up with a better place to meet?"

"Um . . . ," Becky said, "how about *any*where else?"

"Brilliant," I said. "That's a brilliant and creative suggestion."

I went over to the vending machine and got a Coke and a bag of Fritos and then sat back in one of the rolling metal baskets and hung my legs over the side. And Becky did the same. She fiddled with her nose ring and then held her hand out for the Coke and I passed it to her.

"Remember when we put Declan in the dryer and turned it on?"

I laughed. A few years ago Declan was shorter than Becky and super skinny and we used to hang out in the

Laundromat eating candy and taking turns going for a spin in the dryer. But once we got more into skateboarding and could drive we didn't hang out there anymore. We'd get high and walk out to Friendly's and eat ice cream and then skate in the parking lot until they kicked us out.

But I still liked the Laundromat; there was something about it that reminded me of simpler times and I liked to go there to just watch people or think. When I was little sometimes my parents weren't home to make dinner because of work and I'd get change out of the big jar in the living room and walk down to the Laundromat and get lots of candy from the vending machine and sit there, watching people do their laundry. It was kinda comforting just watching people fold clothes as the sun was going down. I didn't usually know them, they were just adults doing household stuff and it was nice to talk to them sometimes. Like we kept each other company. I remember one time my parents came home and couldn't find me and I was at the Laundromat. After that Ally got all freaked-out about me going there and told me to stay home. Anyway. It was a place I came sometimes to clear my head a little when things got stressful or confusing.

"It's so fucked-up about Brian," Becky said. She'd been really worried about the kid and I guess the whole town was and maybe that's why we were back there eating junk food and sitting in the rolling baskets. Maybe it made the town feel normal and boring again. Or it would have felt normal and boring if there weren't Missing posters with Brian's picture on them hanging on the bulletin board. What had happened was starting to change us. Make us grow up a little I guess.

"Maybe we can do something to help find him," I said.

"Listen, Tate," Becky said. "Don't even start in about Graham being some kind of stalker creep child molester or something. He made one of those films of me and I'm fine, and besides, you said the cops were already over at his house. If there was something to find, don't you think they would have?"

"No, no, no. I know, I'm not saying he kidnapped Brian. I'm saying maybe we can help find who did it. Graham talked a lot to the kid. Maybe he knows something or figured something out, some clue."

I was thinking about this one time me, Becky, and Declan hitchhiked far out into the country and pretended we were lost and then knocked on people's doors to ask them for directions. We weren't lost. I don't know why we did it. We were just curious about what the insides of people's houses looked like. And as usual we were bored out of our minds.

This got me thinking about how the cops would be searching for Brian.

"Hey, that's it!" I said.

"What's it?" Becky said with a mouth full of Fritos.

"We'll do the 'We're lost, can we use your bathroom?' thing."

"You really think this is the time to do something like

that? God, Tate, stick with something. I thought you wanted to try to find Brian."

"Duh. This *is* how I want to try to find him," I said. "The cops can only cover so much ground and regular people aren't allowed to snoop around people's houses."

"You want to go looking for a missing kid by walking into people's houses? Why are you so crazy? I mean, really, do you even know why you are so crazy?"

"It's not crazy, Becks. Better yet, we can be all like, *Hey, I'm lost, can we use your computer to email my mom*, and then we check what websites they've been on."

"So okay, we're going into the house of someone who may, like, molest or kidnap kids. That's a place we're trying to get *into*? And they're just going to let us on their computers based on a really, really dumb idea."

I said, "It's worth a try. Otherwise we just sit around here feeling weird and freaked-out, and I am not about feeling weird and freaked-out."

She sighed and drank more of the Coke and then looked again at the Missing picture. He was wearing his X-Men T-shirt in it and smiling. Becky's eyes filled with tears.

I reached over and held her hand. "What is he like?"

She shrugged. "He used to come with his mom and hang out and read comics when she was cleaning. I remember he was really sweet. He came up to my room once and I showed him how to make things on the computer. We used to get him to talk about stuff because he had such a cute little voice.

I dunno. I always thought he was a cool little kid, you know?"

"IS a cool little kid," I said. "And we can help look for him."

"Okay. Yeah." Becky's voice was hoarse and she wiped her eyes. "It's better than doing nothing. Do you think Graham can really help with this?"

I nodded. I didn't tell her about all the feelings I had about Graham or about the fact that he was already trying to get with Ally. My feelings about him were all mixed-up. But if there was a chance to help this little kid I was going to take it.

If there's one thing I'm good at it's taking chances.

SYD

DECLAN

BECKY

GRAHAM

We left the Laundromat and walked through the winding roads back into our neighborhood and headed to Declan's. I remember feeling like we had a sense of purpose at last. Not just about finding Brian, but in general. I remember thinking that Brian going missing somehow revealed what our lives were really like. We generally didn't do much. We listened to music and skated and went to school and got stoned. Sometimes my parents decided I should go sailing with them or go to a party.

I suddenly had this sense that maybe all the nothing we did wasn't really our fault. The cutting class and doing nothing and sitting in the Laundromat or at the beach or out in the woods just waiting for whatever—waiting for our lives to begin. Those things weren't entirely because we were bad kids. It's just that there wasn't much to do unless you were like Ally and got a kick out of baking muffins. There was a whole world out there that we were going to inherit and it wasn't a very good one.

I know Ally saw the good in everything—even in the end she saw the good in everything. But me, I wanted to change things so that when I finally got out of Rockland and made my own way it would be in a better place. The problem was I didn't know how to do it. And every time I felt like I might be figuring it out something came up that swept it all away. It might not be our fault we were like this, but we were the only ones who could do anything to change it. If we wanted things to be better we had to do it. We had to work together and do it. The AMBER Alert for Brian and everyone coming together made me feel something I had never felt before and that was part of a community. Part of a big group of people who look out for one another.

That evening with Becky and Declan, I felt like we were good people. Like we were the children of this town and we were trying to help other children in the town. The adults may not be doing a great job all the time and some of them were probably actually dangerous. But other people were doing so much and felt so touched and hurt by what happened. It was all one more thing that made me want to change. Made me want to understand Ally, made me want to do what Richards wanted. I guess when Brian went missing it was another turning point for me. Made me think in ways I never had or never had to before.

Declan was sitting on his porch waiting for us. His

house was an enormous rambling Victorian with stained-glass windows, a porch swing, and several comfortable wicker chairs scattered about the overgrown lawn, which was full of wildflowers. As usual he was sitting on the floor on the porch surrounded by a pile of books, looking like he didn't even notice us until we were standing right in front of him. And at that point he said, "Greetings, earth women. According to your eight texts, a Facebook chat, and five voice mails, we are endeavoring to discover some information from a handsome arty dullard about a sweet little boy."

Becky rolled her eyes and shook her head. But when Declan looked up he looked serious and worried.

"That's correct," I said.

"Sadly," he went on, "I am preoccupied with some reading for my AP history class, which I have not attended in some weeks. So I don't know that I'll be all that much help."

"Of course you will," I said. "Ditch the studying for tonight. We're just going to go over and see if Graham has any movies of Brian that might help us out and then maybe go around and do the fake 'We're lost' thing so we can get more information."

"The fake-lost thing might be a challenge," he said. "But I'm up for screening the handsome Art Dullard's movies. Let's go." He grabbed his jean jacket off the back of the chair, slipped his bare feet into his black Vans, brushed his long black hair out of his eyes.

"Can you guys not call him Art Dullard?" Becky asked.

"Why?" we said in unison. Then, "Jinx," which we also said in unison.

"Because he's cool as hell, that's why. And he's going to help us."

"Fair enough," said Declan. "I'll let up on the nicknaming until we have further information about his character and intentions."

We walked through the neighborhood and even though we had a purpose and Declan had been trying to keep things light with his usual joking around, things felt terribly heavy and sad. I could tell Becky was having a hard time not thinking about Brian. And I knew the three of us had probably pictured some awful thing happening to him.

When we got back to my driveway, we expected to see Graham on the other side tinkering around in the garage with the Austin. But he wasn't there so we rang the doorbell.

A tall very handsome old guy—Graham's dad, David—answered the door. And smiled.

"Is Graham home?" I asked.

"Oh, hey, Tate, sure, just a minute." He took out his phone and texted something, then asked us to come into the house. Apparently yelling up the stairs wasn't done around here—or maybe Graham just wouldn't be able to hear him. We stood in the front hall and looked around. As usual the massive weird paintings by Graham's stepmom, Kim, seemed to take up all the space around us.

"Would you guys like something to drink? Or a snack?" David asked. He had sweet kind worried-looking eyes.

I said, "No thanks," thinking about all the junk food we'd eaten earlier.

But Becky said, "Yes please," at the same time. Then his phone buzzed and he looked at it. "Graham will be right down. I'll go get some refreshments."

When David headed down the hall to the kitchen, Kim came around the corner holding a glass of wine. She was wearing khaki pants with paint all over them and a man's button-down shirt. Her hair was up in a loose bun. She smiled when she saw us standing there. I remember thinking how smart she looked. Like she had a look on her face where she seemed to understand everything that was going on and to be deep in thought. Studying us as we stood there.

"Hi, Tate," she said. And then she reached out to shake Becky's hand. "I'm Kim," she said. She nodded at Declan.

These people were very different from other people's parents that I knew. They seemed somehow more there. They really looked at you and asked you questions. And they seemed to be very concerned, but they also treated you like an adult, didn't ask a bunch of silly questions about school but just talked about regular stuff.

Graham's dad came out of the kitchen with a plate that had fancy crackers and cheese on it and a bowl full of tiny black olives. He set it on the coffee table in the living room and then pulled three little bottles of San Pellegrino from the pocket of his sports jacket and handed them to us. We sat in a row on the couch under Kim's massive painting of a jellyfish. The house was so immaculately clean and bright and smelled good. I remember thinking how weird it was that this place was right next door to my own house, which felt more cavernous and dark and dusty, like the hold of an antique ship. And except for the rooms where Mom entertained historical society people, it was always filled with one construction project or another. Pretty much the only thing that made my house feel like a home was the smell of the muffins Ally baked all the time.

We were not used to this kind of snack or this kind of hospitality from adults and it was like I could hear Becky's voice in my head saying, "See? They are so cool," but that's probably because she said it about Graham once an hour.

David sat down across from us and Kim stood in front of the bookcase near their grand piano, still holding her wine. And then Graham came downstairs looking like he'd escaped from some completely other world. His hair messy, his expression slightly dazed, his clothes rumpled. He looked high.

"Looks like someone's been making art," Kim said. "He's got the unmistakable halo of creation about him."

Graham laughed and looked a little embarrassed. He took a couple olives out of the bowl and popped them into his mouth.

"You guys want to come upstairs?" he asked.

"Yeah."

David said, "We're ordering Thai food later—is there anything special you'd like us to get?"

Declan and Becky and I looked at each other. We didn't even know you could order Thai food in Rockland. Or really what it even was.

"Maybe just four pad thais?" Graham said.

"Gotcha," his dad said, and nodded.

"Could we eat it in the screening room?" Declan asked.

"Of course," Kim said. "Wherever you're going to be working, we'll bring it up."

I remember thinking how funny it was Kim thought we would be working on something instead of just hanging out. She thought of everything as some kind of art project or the planning for some kind of art project. But actually I guess we would be working. Strategizing, and even I had to admit it was very cool of them to see it that way.

Graham grabbed the bowl of olives and we followed him upstairs. Through the maze of rooms and hallways into his back bedroom.

"What's up, you guys?"

"Not much," I said. "You've heard about Brian, right?"

He nodded. "Yeah, it's so messed up. I was just talking to him last week."

Becky said, "That's why we're here. We thought maybe you had something on your film that would be a clue. You filmed a lot at that park, right?"

"Yeah, and at the school and all around there. You're right. I didn't even think there might be something on the films."

"Can we watch them?" Declan asked.

"Hell yeah!" he said.

We sat on the floor in his room and he opened his Mac Air and looked at it for several minutes. "Yeah, okay, all the files are here. And the raw stuff before I edited it into the main movie. Let's take this to the screening room."

We followed him down another long hallway to the back stairs and then went up to the third floor, to the tiny dark theater where Declan and I had first seen his work and where Declan had first got the idea to christen him "Art Dullard."

But now we were all nervous and anxious to see the movies. I really felt like we were going to find Brian's kidnapper. That Graham might have even captured him on film. Graham attached his laptop to the projector and then Brian's soft round face filled the screen. Becky took a sharp breath and then started crying.

"What are you up to?" Graham's voice asked on the audio.

"I'm headed to Professor Xavier's house," Brian said.

"Oh yeah? What are you going to do there?"

"Meet up with my friends, because we all have the X-Gene."

"You're an X-Man?"

Brian nodded and held out his arm for the camera to inspect. He had drawn the word *X-Man* on himself in magic marker.

Graham's voice said, "That's awesome, dude."

In the background when the camera pans back you can see there are several people sitting in the park. A guy reading the newspaper, a couple walking past, Brian's mother and baby sister perched on a bench across the way.

"Wait," Declan said. "Go back and pause it."

Graham did and we looked at a guy wearing a blue sweat suit, who seemed to be looking right at Brian as he walked past.

"What time is that on the footage?"

"Four forty-three," Graham said.

Declan pulled a little notebook out of his pocket and wrote something down. We did that for every part of the film where some stranger appeared or someone seemed to be looking at Brian.

The film was just Graham talking to Brian. Asking him questions that were the little-kid version of what he had asked Becky when he filmed her.

"Where do you live? How old are you? What's your favorite food? What's your favorite show? Where do you go to school? Where do you like to play? Do you have any brothers or sisters?"

All his answers were kinda cute and funny because he had a squeaky voice and he talked a lot—for every answer he would practically give his whole life story.

"My mom used to pick me up because she was working, but now she's home with the baby and I walk home by myself and have to be really quiet because she's taking a nap but usually my mom takes a nap too before our gramma gets there and then she has to go to work again. I can even go home by myself when no one's there. I'm Wolverine."

"How do you get home from school?" Graham asked.

"I take Sunnyside Drive and then my friends keep going to Demerest Parkway and I turn down Hendy Creek by myself."

"Do you ever walk along the creek?"

"Sometimes."

Declan and I exchanged looks. I knew he was thinking what I was thinking. I felt my heart pounding and like I was going to throw up.

"Wait," I said. "Wait a minute. Who besides us has seen this movie?"

Graham shrugged. "Anybody can buy it from my site."

"*What?*" Becky asked, suddenly shocked.

"I have a site and you can buy any of my stuff about Rockland or my experimental stuff; once the payment processes, the file downloads. I told you, people have spent hundreds of dollars, sometimes more, for my films. I wasn't lying. I need to make money so I can do my major feature-length film."

Declan looked like he was going to be sick. "Graham,"

he said. "Do you know who downloads the films—is there a record?"

"I guess. It's all through PayPal and my Amazon wish list. People buy me things from my wish list and then they get the movie. The ones of kids talking are pretty popular because I guess everyone loves kids. I actually thought I'd film Brian for a long time—like over his life, so you can see how he changes. Like in the documentary *35 Up*. Have you seen it?"

"Graham," Becky said, her voice shaking. "This movie has all of Brian's personal information in it."

"I know. It's amazing how much he talks."

"No," she said. "I mean, you sold this thing and it has the kid's address and everything on it."

"Yours does too," he said. Still seeming not to get it.

Becky glanced at me with incredulous fury and was about to say something to Graham but Declan cut her off.

"We have to take this to the police and find out who downloaded the movie," Declan said.

Then Graham started to look freaked-out. "Oh my God, no way! We cannot take any of this to the police."

"We *have* to!" I shouted. "Are you crazy? This kid could be out there and maybe they could find him right away because of this."

Graham stood up and started pacing around.

"No," he said. "No way. I didn't do this so someone would hurt Brian. This is just a movie."

"Didn't you ever wonder why so many people were buying your movies?" Declan asked.

"Because they're good!" Graham said. Then he looked sheepish and shrugged like maybe he did know. "Whatever," he said defensively. "This is my job and my art; I'm not going to go to the police and have them take everything away from me. This is just what happened with the stuff me and Eric made. Why can't people understand art when they see it?"

Declan and I exchanged shocked looks.

"What kind of movies did you and Eric make?" Declan asked.

"Beautiful movies," he said. "Beautiful, beautiful movies."

ALLY

He called me in the middle of the night and his voice was rough with sleep or sleeplessness.

"You can't let them do this to me," he said. "You understand how I feel and what I'm doing. I don't know why everyone tries to blame me for the things that go wrong."

"Shhh," I whispered into the phone, and then slipped out of bed and into the bathroom so I could have more privacy. "What's going on?"

"You can't let them take this stuff to the police. I had nothing to do with what happened to Brian."

"Shh. Shh. Shh. It's okay."

"Meet me outside," he said. "Down in my backyard by the fountain."

I would have said no but he sounded so upset and frightened I agreed. "Okay," I said. "Ten minutes."

I had never done anything like this in my life but I had

never heard someone sound so afraid before. I put on my sweatshirt and wool socks, then grabbed my shoes and carried them down the stairs so I wouldn't make noise. Then I crept quietly over the creaky floors to the back door and slipped out.

The sky was a deep black-blue and stars shone brightly down. The moon was a little silver crescent. I could see him already beneath the fountain staring into the woods. He was wearing a black hoodie with a flannel shirt under it and his same Diesel jeans. He had a blanket wrapped around his shoulders. The water in the fountain was burbling. It shone liquid and lovely in the starlight. Even though he was upset and I was doing something I shouldn't be doing I had an incredible sense of freedom being outside in secret with no one around.

When he saw me, he ran forward and held me in his arms. Rested his head on my shoulder. I could feel how much he needed to be hugged and we stood that way for a long time.

"What's going on?" I said finally.

He looked at me annoyed and confused for a moment and then shook his head. "Please, you have to know I had nothing to do with anything bad that may have happened to Brian. I thought he was a nice kid and a really interesting subject."

I laughed a little at the way he said it. "Yeah," I said. "I know you did."

"Don't let Declan and Becky go to the police."

"I can't make Syd and her friends do anything," I said.

He held both my hands and squeezed them and looked intently into my face.

"You can, though. You can influence her. You can talk to her. Listen, you and me understand each other. I know we do. We know what it's like to be shy and outside and different and see things that other people don't."

He was staring at me so intensely and his face was beautiful and pale in the starlight. His cheeks were flushed and his eyes looked dark and frightened like an animal's.

"I don't know anything about this," I said. "If you have some information the police need maybe you could just give it to them yourself. You can explain that you were working on this documentary. You just give them what you have. I don't think they would take it away from you."

He looked like he was thinking about it. "I'm afraid," he said.

"Don't be afraid. People know you don't mean any harm. You could be a hero." I watched a wave of relief pass over his face.

"I don't know how I got to have you in my life," he said. And then he held me and kissed me. He laid the blanket down in the dewy leaf-strewn grass and then we lay down together beside the burbling fountain. He put his hands inside my sweatshirt and I held his head and kissed him.

Being beside him, and taking care of him that way,

made my heart race and when he pressed himself against me I did not say no. I did not push him away. I held him tight and felt our hearts beating in unison. Felt our hearts beating as one. And I knew then I would protect him. Just like I had always protected Syd.

When I slipped back into my room at three a.m. she was awake. Sitting up in bed with her arms folded.

"Where were you?"

"I went for a walk," I said. Already feeling like this was some kind of weird role reversal.

"A walk into Graham's backyard?"

I could feel my face flushing. She took Sparkle Pig from her bed and threw it at me. "What the hell are you doing, Ally? What is going on?"

"Graham's worried you and your friends are going to report him to the police."

"Don't you ever wonder why he is so freaked-out about the police?"

"No," I said. "Lots of people are freaked-out by the police. You and your pothead friends are freaked-out by the police."

"Don't you wonder why he goes to school only when he feels like it and he's always hanging around with his cameras and he acts so spaced-out?"

"We both know the answers to those questions," I said simply. I was not going to get into her hysterical immature way of being. And frankly I didn't care. It might have been one of the most special nights of my life and I wasn't going to let her ruin it with her negative way of thinking.

"Ally," she said. "I'm worried about you. Graham has made a bunch of weird movies and he doesn't think there's anything wrong with them or with selling them to strangers online. He made one of Brian and he made one of Becky and God knows who else. We watched some of them yesterday and thinking that anyone could get ahold of these is really scary."

"It's no different than Facebook," I said. "It's the same as having a Tumblr account." Which were things I had heard Graham say before.

"It's very different from Facebook," Syd said.

"Listen," I said. "He knows what the right thing to do is and he'll do it. It's not up to us to go to the police or mess with his life."

"Oh my God, Ally! It's totally up to us. If we have information and we do nothing about it and something happens to Brian, it will be our fault too. We will have helped the person who took him."

"That's assuming the person who took him had any knowledge of Graham's movies, which they probably didn't."

"But even if there is only the slightest chance they did, it should be reported."

"He's going to go to the police himself."

"What? How do you know?" Syd asked.

"Because I asked him to," I said simply. "Because he knows it's the right thing to do. You can't blame him for being scared. After the way his whole life was turned upside down."

"How was his whole life turned upside down?" she asked. "I don't think anyone has any clue what happened in Virginia."

"I have a clue," I said quietly

"What?" she whispered fiercely. "Ally, tell me."

"He and Eric made some movies and they got in trouble for it. The same kind of thing I guess where they were young and Eric's family thought the movies were really offensive. Also they were filming and not paying attention and they crashed the Austin. I think actually they may have crashed the Austin on purpose because of how it would look on film and then that's where all the trouble started. After that they found all the other movies and Eric's family made a big deal of it and sued Graham's family and they haven't seen each other since even though they were friends since they were three. Can you imagine not being able to talk to Becky ever again?"

"Yes, okay, I get that some weird shit happened, but what were the movies? Do you think they were . . . Do you think they were like porn or something?" Even as she said it, I could see it interested her more than disgusted her.

"No," I said. "I don't. He's too shy, you don't know him like I do. I think they were probably something as silly as

Becky smoking or Brian talking about X-Men. Just nothing. He said they thought they were making something that expressed how beautiful life was, but people twisted it the wrong way. He said he has only one copy of the movie left that no one knows about and he's going to make it part of a bigger movie and then sell it—maybe get an art agent or a gallery interested in his stuff. But he's had to hide all these things and if he had to go to the police, it would ruin everything he's worked for and get him in more trouble and probably make his parents take his camera away."

She was very quiet, thinking. I came over and lay on her bed next to her. She wasn't really mad. We were both exhausted and I was flushed with the joy of being with Graham; I could still feel the amazing warmth of his skin against mine. I sighed and she ran her fingers through my hair.

"Ally," she said. "He didn't make one of those movies of you, did he?"

"It doesn't matter," I whispered, exasperated at her questions. "It doesn't matter if he did. They're just movies. They're art. They're documenting our lives. Everybody with a Twitter account does the same thing."

I looked up at her and saw her concerned face. Neither of us had the energy for another fight. She was quiet, lost in thought. But when she spoke again she only said, "I'm sorry I threw Sparkle Pig."

I said, "That's okay. It's better than when you stabbed

him with the sewing scissors."

"He needed surgery," she said, starting to laugh a little. "He needed weight-loss surgery."

And then I don't know why but I just threw my arms around her and squeezed her tight. I said, "I love you, Syd."

"Oh God," she said, rolling her eyes. "Hey, what's this about? Why are you all sentimental? Are you getting your period?" Then she looked down into my face. "Oh . . . my . . . God," she said slowly. "Did you and Graham . . . ? Did you?"

I nodded and she smiled a confused smile at me and shook her head and then she kissed me on top of my head. "I love you too, Ally, and I know you're in love." She was silent for a time, and then she said, "But please. Don't let him come between us."

POLICE CHIEF BILL WERTZ

He came in at about seven thirty in the morning, looking restless and unwashed, but dressed like some kind of movie star. Like he could buy the whole town. And he didn't act like any kid his age. He was distant and confident. Someone used to telling people what to do—or at least getting what he asked for.

He had a laptop computer with him and he said he had something to show me. Something that might help people find Brian Phillips.

I knew about this kid. I got a buddy in Virginia sent me a juvenile file on him. And I know he had been in some serious trouble. I guess you'd call it serious trouble. It was either trouble or tragedy—so I was ready for something screwy the minute he opened his mouth.

I had him come into the interrogation room, fully expecting him to confess to something I did not want to hear. In a case like a missing child you have no time to spare. You get answers as fast as you can and you make sure you get the details. He wasn't with his parents or a lawyer, so I was pretty sure we could get him talking. We'd had two days of dead ends and hell looking for Brian, and his mother's worry was weighing on everyone. Heartbreaking.

He opened the little computer and then clicked on a file and a movie of Brian came up.

"What the hell is this?" I asked.

"I'm making a documentary about the town and I have footage of Brian talking. I posted this online and I think someone may have seen it and used it to kidnap him."

The words were like a punch to the gut. I was infuriated with this rich little prick, and at the same time I knew this was the strongest lead we had on the case.

"Do you know who's seen it?" I asked.

"A lot of people," he said. "I have these names, but I don't know if they're the people's real names or not." He handed me a piece of paper with a list of names on them.

And I straightaway handed it to Evans. "Check these names against the sex offender registry," I told him. And I could see the kid cringe even as I said it.

"I didn't mean any harm," he said. I looked at him. I don't know if I believed him or not. I'd read his file and I knew what he'd said to the judge back in Virginia and I saw how his parents' money and connections made that case just disappear quietly. But he was still a kid. He thought like a kid—no sense of any consequences.

I said, "Graham, I'm going to need to see the website where you've got this stuff posted."

"Of course," he said. He called it up on his computer and he also wrote down the web address.

Just as I was bending down to look at it, Evans yelled, "We got a hit!"

Everyone in the office stood as if they were shocked into motion.

I told Evans, "Get me a location on that right away." And I told Graham, "You sit tight for a minute, you might be able to help us out. Was there a credit card used to buy the movie? Or a phone number? If there is, we can track him."

"Not that I could see," he said. "He got the movie in exchange for buying me something on my Amazon wish list as a gift—so I couldn't see any of his information except the name. He wrote his name and then just the word *thanks*. Once the Amazon sale is shipped the movie uploads. I set it all up automatically and I almost never see a name or real information."

I shook my head, disgusted at the way kids lived today. What ever happened to playing ball in the park or getting a job after school?

"What did he buy you?" I asked, assuming it would be some books or music.

When he told me, my jaw dropped. It was a six-hundred-dollar camera with an optical zoom lens. I don't need to tell you how much trouble a kid could be in for selling a movie to a registered pedophile, who in turn bought him a sophisticated surveillance camera.

"Graham," I said. "I think you should wait right here and we'll call your parents." As I was picking up the phone to call them, Evans shouted, "We got a location!"

We didn't have enough men on staff to babysit rich boy while we tried to take down the scumbag that kidnapped Brian Phillips. The fact that he'd bought the movie and that he was on the registry was enough for a search warrant. Talking to Graham would have to wait. Rockland was a small force and we had no excuse to hold a kid who had just brought us this information voluntarily.

"Go!" I shouted. "Get moving." I grabbed my jacket and headed out to the lot with the unmarked cars. "Graham, you go home and stay home. We'll contact you later to ask you some questions."

He looked astonished. "Did you find him? You found him already?" He laughed a little to himself.

I ushered him out the door. And ducked into the car. "We don't know if we've found him or not. We'll call you," I said. We sped out and left him standing there.

I was, of course, terrified that we would be too late. It had been two days and the name we had was of a man who had already served time for taking a little girl down in Portland on a ten-day drive. Usually people like this feel they got nothing to lose if they're going to do it again.

The house was way out by Chickawaukie Pond, near Achorn Cemetery, and I had to stop myself from thinking the worst. From thinking that little boy was already in the pond or dumped in Glen Cove.

We surrounded the house with the full force and backup from Waldoboro. I could feel him standing on the other side of the door when we rang the bell. I could feel him waiting, thinking we'd go away if he waited. He was trapped.

We pounded again and he opened the door. The place was neat and orderly—too orderly, like a hotel room.

I said, "We'd like to ask you a few questions about Brian Phillips, the boy who disappeared in Rockland last week. We understand you bought a movie that was made of him."

His eyes darted just briefly toward a door off the kitchen when I said Brian's name, and I motioned to Evans to check it out.

He took two uniforms with him, tramping down a flight of stairs while I questioned the scumbag about where he'd been the last four days. And soon I heard them calling up to us, telling us to call in an ambulance. Then they came rushing upstairs, Evans carrying Brian. He was unconscious and his hands and feet were tied.

I had the uniforms handcuff the scumbag and take him out to the car. I wanted to kick the living shit out of him right there but I knew he'd be getting plenty of that in prison.

Evans sat in a chair at the kitchen table and I cut away

the ropes that tied Brian. From the way he was breathing, I was certain that he had been drugged. His pulse was slow and steady, and apart from some bruises and chapped lips, he looked okay. He must have been terrified and dehydrated, and clearly other things had happened to him or were about to happen to him before we arrived.

It was one of the quickest recoveries of an abducted child in the history of the state. We called Brian's mother right there from the house and told her that her boy was found and seemed fine but needed to go to the hospital. And I'll never forget the way she exhaled and started crying and laughing on the phone. As if she'd been holding her breath for days.

Evans held the boy close to his chest and we all felt like we had won the lottery.

On the way back to the car one of the uniforms said, "If that kid Graham hadn't come in we might not have found him."

I shook my head. "If that kid Graham wasn't out making his movies, Brian would have been home with his mom and baby sister this whole time."

But what he said was true. It took guts for a teenager with his history to come in and turn that information over to us. And thank God he did.

At least one tragedy was averted that year. At least one.

SYD

So Graham was officially a hero. Story in the paper and the whole thing.

"Art Dullard might have been too stupid to even know that what he did was connected to Brian's kidnapping," Declan said on the way to school. "If you hadn't made us go over there and convince him, God knows what would have happened."

"Yeah, well, it was Becky who said we should get him to help, and he did."

"I don't understand," Declan said. "He was dead set against anyone finding out, and then he went there himself."

I shrugged. But I knew exactly why he turned over the movies to the cops. Ally had convinced him in her gentle way. He wanted her to think of him as a hero and she could be very convincing sometimes. I don't think he would have done it if he wasn't afraid we'd do it ourselves and if he didn't have Ally persuading him. It was a one-two punch from the Tate sisters.

"He still doesn't think he did anything wrong," I said. "You can tell he just doesn't understand these things."

"Yeah," he said. "But you can also tell he's kind of our friend now too. We didn't rat him out that night. We went to bed and in the morning he did it himself. We ate pad thai at his house and talked to him like he was our friend. I think he's our friend, Tate."

I sighed. The mystery of Graham wasn't that he had stupidly sold information to pedophiles. There was something more going on. Maybe I could sense these things because my own life was not exactly what it seemed all the time. Maybe I knew because he seemed like two different people to Ally and me when we talked to him.

But no matter how you cut it I knew. And it didn't help things that people now thought he was a hero. Or the newspaper did at any rate. The creep who took Brian had I guess manipulated Graham too somehow. I don't think he'd have given that information to someone doing bad things. But then again maybe he would. When we asked him about it the night we watched the movies, he didn't seem to care why these people were paying so much for the movies. According to the newspaper, he didn't tell the cops the same story he told us. Just that the guy had bought him a camera—not paid him money. Unless there were more people who bought the movies that we didn't know about.

Everything seemed to be getting more complicated, not less. What did it mean that even Declan thought he was our friend?

"C'mon, Tate," Declan said. "Don't you think you're being a little hard on him because you have a crush on him?"

"Why does everyone keep saying that?" I asked.

"Well . . . because it looks that way. The way you were hanging out with him after school and stuff."

"What the hell are you talking about? It sounds like you're the one who's jealous."

He laughed. "Of Art Dullard? No. But he is there—right next door and always around—and I could see how you might be interested in him."

"Becky's the one with the crush."

"Right," he said. "Becky and everyone else. I'm just a dope-smoking brainiac with long black hair."

"Me too," I said.

He laughed and then he stopped walking and stood in front of me.

"I love you, Earthling," he said.

I was surprised he said it. We were close and I knew we loved each other but we didn't talk like this. First Ally telling me she loves me and now this. Everyone was getting soft on me.

"Declan, what the hell?"

"I mean it. The way you took charge of this situation and

made us go over there. The way you convinced him. You're really changing. You get cooler and more badass and more responsible every day." He laughed. "How can you be such a bad girl and such a good girl at the same time?"

"Good role models, I guess."

Then he bent down and kissed me and I held him tight and for some reason I felt like I might cry.

GRAHAM

Dear Lined Piece of Paper,

What a week. No sooner had I figured out a way to finance my fantastic project than it has been taken away. At least temporarily. Brian—the X-Man kid who I had hoped to do a long-term film project about—was found. I guess I should say he was kidnapped. Yes. He was kidnapped and then found in some guy's basement. The guy had bought the movie I made about Brian, and so he knew some things that made it easier to take him.

Man. People do some fucked-up things. I'm glad he's back, but I doubt his parents will let me make any more movies of him. The police called after he was found, and they wanted to talk to me about my website and the movies, but Dad and Kim said I don't have to talk to anyone, and they got our lawyer to explain things to them. Brian's family is happy he's home, and they think the movies I made saved his life! So no one is there to press any charges at all.

And you know what? It did save his life, just like Tate said it would.

Oh God, Tate. I can hardly think about her now without feeling butterflies in my stomach. I keep remembering her out on the lawn by the fountain holding me in her arms and whispering so sweetly and making everything better. She's the most interesting person I have ever known. I've been watching the movie I took of it all week. There's no sound, which makes it even better. I used the little camera and attached it to the edge of the fountain. So you can't see all of us, mostly just our faces and chests. She's so beautiful. I need to have her over to make more movies of her in my room. I like it when she talks about her life. I like how she changes and how her expressions are so free floating. I like everything about her.

I want her to be the star of the best movie I have ever made. Something better than what Eric and I made. Something that really will reveal all the beauty in the world.

I had to talk to Dr. Adams again about Brian. He asked me how I felt and I told him I felt like I had corrected something that went wrong before and also afraid that it might mean my camera would be taken away.

He said, "What would it mean if your camera was taken away?" And before I even realized what I was saying I said, "It would mean that I was blind."

"Can't you see without your camera?" he asked.

I said yes I can but I was really thinking no. I totally can't. Of course not. Not the way I want to. Not the way I need to, so I can study things and understand what's going on. No, actually not at all! I would rather look at a movie I've made of myself than look in the mirror, because it's more interesting. If I have a movie of Tate, I can rewatch it and understand what's going on. It doesn't slip away through time into nowhere.

But of course I said yes. Sure, I would still be able to see blah blah blah. And I didn't tell him about correcting my own dosages. I didn't tell him that actually I was mad at Brian for getting kidnapped because he almost got my camera taken away from me. He almost made me blind.

If it wasn't for Tate figuring out it would be better for me to go to the police myself I'd be completely screwed.

KIM

We should have known something was wrong. We should have known he was struggling. I do blame myself for this. The fact was we had a lot of time at home with him and we spent a lot of time together, the three of us.

David essentially left his job so he could be a better father and be there for Graham, and I know I was the one who constantly reassured him that there was no problem.

When the police called and said a film Graham had made was probably the reason Brian Phillips was kidnapped, I told them the one sure thing was that a film Graham made was the reason Brian Phillips was saved. Then they told me about the wish list and the camera. A known pedophile had bought Graham a camera. And Graham had provided this person with our home address, where the camera was shipped. That startled me. So many strangers having our address. I know kids think differently about privacy than we did when we were young. But this was a serious lack of judgment.

"Why would you do that?" we asked him. "If you wanted a different lens or a different camera, why wouldn't you ask us?"

He said he wanted his movie to be a surprise. He wanted to be independent. He thought no one would trust him after what happened in Virginia. And all those things seemed reasonable. Heartbreakingly reasonable conclusions for a young boy to come to.

Dr. Adams said it was important to have consequences, but at this point I still believed it was wrong, completely wrong, to take the camera away. I thought it would only make him do something more desperate in order to have it. I understood how important it was to him to have it—to be able to control his environment more, to frame what he saw and what he looked at again. I felt I understood him.

The consequences we gave him had to do with the car. No more driving the Austin to school, and David was putting the new car—the one they were planning to work on together next—on hold. He wouldn't have it shipped until things settled down.

"What do you mean by *settled down*?" Graham shouted at us. "You take everything from me. First I can't see Eric, then I can't watch my own movies, now I can't put things on my wish list or drive my own car. And you won't let me work on the new one you promised me. What am I supposed to do?"

David remained calm and loving, as he always does in these situations. "Well," he said, "it seems like you've got a nice group of friends here, and you're lucky to have folks right next door. Maybe you could spend more time with them. You know, when I was your age, I didn't have a car."

Graham groaned and rolled his eyes. "I know. I know. You've told me. I know. But I thought that's one of the reasons you wanted me to have one."

David told him he was sorry, but it wasn't negotiable.

I remember thinking this would all blow over. I remember thinking this was just a stage he was going through and that eventually he would realize we were right. I remember thinking that once he became more a part of high school and his friends, he'd be more reasonable about these things. I remember thinking a lot of things that fall, and looking back now, none of our ideas would have made any goddamn difference.

DECLAN

was meditating in my backyard. A lot had happened that week, and I was trying to practice having a blank mind so later I could use my powers of concentration to get some work done. Tate and I had been skipping school a lot before all that stuff with Brian happened, and I realized once things had settled down that I was probably not going to be valedictorian. She was. Which was fine and all, but I thought maybe we could get our GPAs so that they were identical. Maybe it could be both of us. Anyway. I was out there relaxing by the fishpond, sitting on a stone slab and trying to naturally expand my consciousness, and when I opened my eyes, Graham Copeland was standing right in front of me with a camera.

I blinked a few times to make sure he wasn't an apparition of some kind. Then I laughed and said, "What's up, G?"

He said, "I'm just out roaming the neighborhood."

"Dude," I said. "How are things going? How does it feel to be a hero?"

"Good," he said. "It feels good to be a hero. I think it's good publicity for my career as a filmmaker."

"Well, there you go," I said. "Hey, can you turn that camera off? We're just having a conversation. I don't think it needs to be documented."

"Oh," he said, looking startled. "Yeah, sure." He turned it off and slid it into his pocket.

"So, how are things?" I asked again. He looked a little weird, and I wanted him to relax.

"I was wondering about Tate," he said.

"Yeah?"

"Are you in love with her?"

"Yeah," I said.

"Is she your girlfriend?"

"Are you asking if I own Tate?"

"No, it's just when you guys came over the other night, she seemed so caught up in everything about you and impressed with you."

"Huh. I dunno, man. Tate gets caught up in a lot of things."

He nodded. "How long have you guys been together?"

"Been friends?" I asked. "Since elementary school."

"What about Becky?"

"What about her?"

"Are you the same kind of friend with Becky?"

"No. Dude, are you interested in dating *Tate*?"

"I . . . yeah, well, we . . ."

"Look, man, I don't care what extracurricular things Tate might do. She's her own person, got it? And you're my friend. Okay? Everything is cool."

He looked really embarrassed. "Okay, but don't you think she's . . . I mean, that family is kinda . . ."

"Interesting? Very. That's why I'm not about to get all freaked-out by teen romance nonsense. Okay? Tate and I are going to go to college together. We have some plans. I know you have your own plans, and that's cool. We all have our own plans. We're all alone when you get right down to it, right?"

"Yeah."

"C'mon, dude, let's go inside, I want to show you this website that's all about fractals."

I got up and stretched and we walked toward the house. It was okay spending time with him. He was still Art Dullard, but he was kind of okay. And I knew that Tate loved me and that we were getting the hell out of Rockland and that someday we'd talk about knowing Graham Copeland, someday he'd probably be famous. You could kinda see it just by looking at him.

SYD

It had been a week since I'd been called down to the office and it felt kinda weird. Up until now there was only one day when I was almost not called down to the office. Fitzgerald did the announcements and then some dipshit Richards-wannabe got on and started calling names. It's generally the usual suspects, with a few kids who you've never heard of thrown in. That day they got through the whole list without saying the word *Tate*. Everyone in homeroom looked at me and then Trombley, my home-room teacher, came over and patted me on the back and everyone clapped. About a minute later Fitzgerald got on the speaker and said, almost like he got how funny it was: "And last but not least, Ms. Tate."

But that was last year. School had only just started a month ago and for the first few weeks I'd had uninterrupted call-downs. You know how they go. "Don't skate in the hall.

Did you call Letorno a fat ass? Smoking on school grounds? Who did that graffiti out by the north entrance? Mr. Blah blah blah says you've got an attitude whatever." But lately I guess they stopped watching every little thing I did, because the days went by and I didn't have to visit with Richards or Mr. Fitz.

Anyway, this might sound weird but I missed seeing Richards, so I took myself to the office. She was wearing a pair of thick black-framed glasses and a black blouse with polka dots and a wide silver bracelet and her hair was up on her head in a bun with a pencil poked through it.

She smiled when I walked in. "What's up, homegirl?"

"Just checking on you," I said.

I'd been away from the office so long the jar of black licorice was gone and she actually had some candy that looked good on her desk—some kind of square gummy stuff covered with sugar. She held out the dish and offered me one and I popped it in my mouth.

Big mistake. "Oh my God, what is *wrong* with you?!" I said, wincing, and spit it into my hand. My whole mouth was burning. "What is that flavor? Cleaning solvent?"

She laughed and took two of the gross torture candies and started chewing them. "It's crystallized ginger," she said.

"Are you sure you're supposed to *eat* it?"

She nodded and ate another one.

"Why can't you just have a jar of M&M's on your desk like a normal authority figure?"

"'Cause that stuff'll kill you," she said. "Sit down. What's new? I haven't seen you in weeks."

A lot was new of course. She had to know from reading the papers what had happened with Brian and Graham.

"My next-door neighbor is a hero, I guess."

She nodded, still chewing on the ginger. "That's what I've been hearing. Did you know he had taken those movies of Brian Phillips?"

I nodded and suddenly felt weird. Realized that maybe this was why I had come down to the office. I guess I wanted to talk about it.

She looked at me for what seemed like a really long time. Then she got up and shut her door.

"What's up?" she said when she sat back down.

"I think it's kinda effed-up," I said.

Richards nodded. "Me too."

"He wasn't going to tell the police about it at all, but we all convinced him to do it. If four other people hadn't been nagging him, he never would have gone to the police in the first place. And he was scared to do it."

"Why was he scared?"

"That's just it, I don't know. And I don't know why we saved his ass instead of telling them we thought something weird was going on. He's made a lot of films of people."

"Has he made one of you?" she asked.

"Not me," I said. "Unless he's done it without me knowing."

I swallowed hard and continued. "And now this hero stuff. I mean, it's so frustrating. Maybe he's a hero somehow, but I guess I just don't know if what I'm thinking is right or if I've made him some kind of monster in my head. Nobody wants to believe someone like him would do anything bad intentionally."

"What do you really think?"

"I think he's a creep. No one else does, but I do, I think there's something weird there. But every time I talk to him he's nicer and cooler to me and I guess we're becoming friends. God, I don't know what to do."

She said, "You've got a good head on your shoulders, Tate. And I think you do know what to do. The main thing is you need to protect yourself. If you think he's made any movies of you or anyone else, you should go to the police."

I nodded. "I'll think about it," I said. "Hey, can you write me a pass? I'm going to be late for chemistry after all this gabbing."

She got out her pink pad and wrote me an excuse. "Don't be a stranger," she said, "and don't start getting in trouble just to come hang out here. You don't have to do that. You can come talk to me any time you want."

"I know," I said. Then I took a few of those gross ginger candies so I could give them to the kid I got stuck with for a lab partner. I'd tell him they were apple-flavored.

BECKY

My family was so happy when Brian Phillips was found. We all were, the whole town. So relieved. My parents gave his mom a raise and started paying for her family's health insurance. I didn't know they had no health insurance, but as my mom said, they would sure need it now.

Brian had to stay in the hospital for a couple days, and then my mom said he was going to need a lot of counseling, but he would be okay. We went to visit him. I brought him a Wolverine action figure. I knew he already had one, but I figured another couldn't hurt.

"I don't really have superpowers," he said when I saw him. We were in his parents' backyard on a narrow little street down by the harbor.

"Me neither," I said.

"What did you think yours were?" he asked.

"I thought my superpowers were that I could tell what

everyone was like by looking at them," I said.

"I thought that too!" Brian said. "And also that I had metal bones and could fight."

"I have real powers, though," I told him.

"What are they?"

"I can hack into computers—I'll show you sometime. What are your real powers?"

"I'm more patient than anyone on earth," he said. "And I can remember everything."

"That means that you actually will have superpowers one day," I told him.

"Really?"

"Pretty much," I said. "Come here, bud." I gave him a big hug. "You have a good memory, but you're forgetting some of your other real powers."

"What are they?"

"You're brave. You're one of the bravest kids I know. You're smart. You're friendly. You're good. You're a very, very good little boy. Those are all real powers."

He jumped a couple of times after I said it and took the Wolverine action figure and threw him and caught him.

I looked up and saw my mom and his mom standing in the window, looking out at us and smiling. And I knew then that we were all friends and that these people were not just people who worked for my family. I was proud of my mom. And for the first time since I was maybe Brian's age, I thought I wanted to be just like her when I grew up.

SYD

There were no other cars in the driveway, and I'd watched him and his stepmom Kim leave about twenty minutes before, carrying her Hermès bag, wearing her Prada boots but still dressed in that weird way she had. Loose jeans covered with paint, her hair tied up in a knot at the back of her head and falling in her face. She looked like she didn't care what anyone thought of her ever. They drove somewhere every Tuesday at four and they were always gone for about two hours—sometimes three.

Once inside the house I realized they were richer than I'd imagined or noticed before. Something about being there alone. The house really was a mansion. I was afraid the minute I got inside that I was in over my head.

The kitchen looked like it came right out of some celebrity chef show. Stainless-steel everything. Everything in the house was at once modern and also somehow antique. Had the feeling of perfection and old money around it. Or at least the kind of money I'd never encountered before. Sure, some kids' parents were doctors or lawyers or had inherited money—but this family seemed loaded in a way that you see on television. They also clearly didn't hire a cleaning lady—even though the place was like a palace it was kind of a mess. Not the way it looked when Declan and Becky and I came over the other day. Books strewn about, papers piled on tables. Half-empty glasses left out with things moldering in their bottoms.

The central staircase was wide and winding and a chandelier hung in the center of the vaulted ceiling. I headed up to Graham's room—quiet as a mouse. His parents' bedroom had a fireplace in it and huge glass-front bookcases. It was the only room in the house that was actually cozy and not filled with some weird art.

There were four rooms upstairs: an art studio, a study lined with books, a room with floor-to-ceiling windows filled with plants, and Graham's room. It was the farthest away from his parents. I expected when I opened the door for the place to be a complete mess like it was when I had seen it before—clothes strewn about the place kind of smelling like boy the way Declan's room smelled. But when I opened it I was shocked. It was pristine. Ordered like some kind of laboratory. Not an article of clothing on the floor. The bed perfectly made. Not a thing out of place on the desk. No crumpled paper, no electronic cables or cords lying around. Nothing. It looked like no one had ever used the room for anything. Like it belonged to a ghost. Like it was a room some parents had perfectly preserved, instead of a place where someone actually lived.

The fact that it was so neat made my heart race. Like he had already cleaned up the scene of a crime. I'd have to remember not to leave a hair out of place or he'd know someone had been in the room. The shelves were filled with DVDs and books. I was again shocked when I realized they were in alphabetical order. I opened his drawers—even the contents were squarely in order. There was a notebook, five identical black pens. A compass and binoculars.

He had two telescopes near the window. A small one and a bigger fancier thing that looked very technical.

I pulled the curtains aside and my blood went cold. The hair on my neck stood up. It was pointed directly at Ally's bed. The placement of the telescope was unmistakable. I had been right. There was no way he wasn't watching her.

I turned on his computer and waited for it to boot up and then I went into the files marked Copeland Productions.

There were so many files I could only hope he was as meticulous in filing them as he was in cleaning his room. I wished Becky was there so that she could just hack right into everything. But she was spending more time with her family and, just like Declan, spending more time studying.

Finally I found it—a folder labeled simply "Allyson." There were dozens of films in it. I figure I'd start with the latest one first—since the other ones were probably creepy things he took from the window before they were really talking.

I clicked on it and a window opened with my face. I was totally shocked. Graham had never interviewed me in his room before. But there I was sitting in the leather chair. I clicked Play. He was asking me questions. And I was shyly answering them. Then he started kissing me.

I watched in horror and fascination, trying to remember when I did this. My heart started pounding. I felt dizzy like I was going to be sick. I felt terrified. There was no way this happened or I would have remembered it. I did not do these things.

I clicked on another and it was me sitting in the passenger seat of Graham's car, my hair blowing in the breeze and laughing. I never went for a drive in Graham's car.

"Are you going to go for another ride with me?" he was asking.

"Of course," Ally's voice said while my lips moved.

"We'll drive out and make movies like me and Eric," he said.

"We'll be stars," Ally's voice said dreamily while my face smiled.

I clicked on another one and it was me talking about baking muffins, wearing Ally's clothes and the pearls she borrowed from Mom, and then I realized it was shot in the hold of Dad's yacht. I haven't been on that yacht since I was in middle school.

Something was terribly wrong. I was freaking out, but then I realized he had simply found a way to transpose my image over hers and use her voice and her answers to the questions he asked her. I can't believe he made it look like we were making out. That was the weirdest part. He must have really liked it that one time we kissed in the garage and just gotten carried away I guess. It looked like he had a whole bunch of films of me but they were all things Ally did and said. Why would he do that? Was this just more of his weird art? It had to be. Or was he doing something creepier like selling this film to some weirdo pervert but making it so they would see my image instead of Ally and go after me?

Graham Copeland was getting stranger and stranger by the second. Just as I was about to click on another movie I heard a door creak downstairs and then footsteps. I quickly logged out of the Ally files and shut down the computer. Then I looked out Graham's window. His father's car was in the driveway. I quickly opened the window and slid out onto the ledge, then pulled myself up onto the roof. I walked over the roof to the back of the house, then hung down and dropped onto the back balcony. Then I hung off the balcony, dropped to the ground, and ran quickly into the woods. My heart pounding in my chest.

I could not believe what I had seen.

SYD

couldn't look at him after I saw that movie. But of course I had to. He lived next door. Our yards were connected. My sister was still in love with him. There were few things as horrible as that. Or at least I didn't yet know how bad things could get.

I decided to talk to Becky about it because she was Junior Hacker Extraordinaire.

She had long since stopped talking to him after the stuff with little Brian.

"It's not that hard to get some spyware on his computer, but finding out stuff that he has buried by using a Trojan horse or trapdoor is going to be really hard."

"Can you do it?"

She looked really uncomfortable. "I *can*. But it's the breaking and entering and doing something illegal that I'm not so into."

"Are you kidding? For this guy?"

"I think we should stay *away* from this guy."

"Can you teach me how to do it?"

She looked at me for a long time, like she was trying to figure out if I was smart enough.

"It's tricky," she said. "I could see you getting frustrated and messing things up."

"Can you make a thing—whatever you said, Trojan horse or secret passage or whatever—can you make one on your computer and then show me how to get into it?"

She nodded. "I can. But listen, I don't want any more part of whatever weird shit is going on with this kid. I'm pissed at him, but honestly, Tate, I'm scared of him. I'm scared of him and then sometimes I think he really is one of our friends and we should try to understand him and make him stop doing weird things. I mean, you know how it is. You're super weird and we love you. Declan's some kind of freaky Buddhist nerd who still studies up in his tree house. Graham's just a little further on the fucked-up scale than we are. I don't think we can figure all this out on our own. I don't think this is something we can do."

"NO?" I shouted. "Then who is going to do it? This guy sold movies of you and Brian and God knows who else to pedophiles! He has weird movies of all of us probably."

"Yeah, but that's not what he was *trying* to do. He thought people just loved his art. He was just stupid."

"Becky! Listen to what you're saying. I don't know if

that's even true, and think about this carefully. When you get right down to it, is there any real difference between stupid and dangerous?"

She sighed. The days of us hanging out and getting high and listening to music and walking around in the woods were over. She was doing full-time computer programming and code writing and making jewelry out of sea glass. What happened to Brian was sobering, except to Declan of course who was never really sober and never really slowed down for anything. All the terrible events didn't make him pause and go back to doing homey things like it had Becky. It made him get high more and study more; he bought Rosetta Stone language courses for Swahili and Cantonese. When I asked him why he said the world was a strange place and knowing how to communicate better meant you had more options to go become a hermit somewhere. So I guess maybe he was kind of affected too in his own way. Had some long-term escape plan going on. But Declan was easy to interest in any kind of investigation.

The problem was I wanted to see the films Graham was hiding but I did not want to discover them with Declan. I was afraid of what we might find. Afraid that there would be worse things or that he had movies of me and my sister that no one should see.

And I wanted to find out what he meant by all this stuff about making movies like he did with Eric—how he was involving my sister in something he had been in serious trouble for. He wanted her to be the new Eric, that was for sure.

I needed to see what else he had. To learn what Becky knew and do it myself.

"Please, Becky, just show me how to do it. I won't involve you in any way. You're not responsible for anything. Besides, you know it's the right thing to do."

She sighed and looked at me again, incredibly sad. Then she reached over and held my hand, saying, "Be careful, Tate."

SYD

got back into the house with no problem. The Copelands for all their wealth and art never locked their windows or had alarms. That's because they were always home. But I was fortunate enough to live next door and be able to see when they all left—to talk to them about where they were going.

I had my chance on Sunday when they all went out to some advance screening of a film Kim's friend had made. They were dressed up and I stood in the driveway talking to them for a few minutes. Graham came out to the car last and he looked high as a kite. I don't know why his parents were so naive and unable to tell he was on drugs but they were. Maybe they just figured that's how people look when they're on Adderall. In any case we talked for some time and then they drove off. I waited for fifteen minutes and then let myself into the house from an open basement window near the back garden. Then quickly made my way back to Graham's room.

I turned on the computer and went back to the main menu of all his movie files. There were so many marked "Allyson" it freaked me out to even think of what he had there. I called up his website, Copeland Productions, and began applying the things Becky told me about so I could break in and see what was behind the shiny arty veneer, what secret movies he might have.

Suddenly, a pop-up appeared asking for an authorization code. I did what Becky showed me and sure enough a whole new page appeared with a much different list and prices written next to each film description. The films were titled "The Girl Next Door" and they all had a number following them; there were "The Girl Next Door" videos volumes 1–70.

The first one I clicked on was of Ally lying in Graham's backyard naked. I gasped. I felt sick. It was terrible to see. It was hard to make out her face in the dark but it was clearly her. We have the same freckles on our chest and a birthmark in the same spot. It was clear she had no idea she was being filmed. I knew I had to get rid of these videos, but I was getting angrier and angrier and felt like I should just get rid of Graham instead.

I logged out of the secret site and made a note of the things I saw there so I could go to the police.

I was about to go but then I thought I should look for

the video he told Ally about. The one of Eric that he said he had hidden. He had a wall of old albums—vinyl—they must have been from his dad's collection like back in the eighties—and a turntable. I don't know why it suddenly hit me but if he was going to hide something he'd hide it in plain sight—a thin little disk slipped into an album would be the perfect hiding spot. It was like I could feel something there calling out to me or maybe I just suspected.

I started pulling albums out and looking at them. And after about fifteen minutes I found it. A DVD slipped out with the vinyl. It was marked with a simple X. Had to be it.

I took it and slid it into his DVD drive and waited.

If there is one thing in the world I regret having done in my life, it is this. If there is one thing I could go back and erase or if I could have made myself blind in the moments before the images came on, I would have. I gladly would have.

The footage was taken from the passenger side of a car going very, very fast. The sun is shining and you can hear laughter. The top is down. It's obviously the Austin. The clouds look like they are flying by overhead and the trees are racing by at the side of the road.

"You make sure you're getting this?" Graham's voice asks.

And then another boy says, "Aw, hell yeah."

"This is going to be our best movie," Graham's voice says again. "This is going to make you a star."

The camera pans over and Graham grins into the lens.

He's wearing dark sunglasses and his cheeks are flushed. He has his seat belt on and he's wearing a helmet.

"This is the life," the other kid says. The road is narrow and hilly and there are no traffic signs; they're out in the country somewhere. In the distance you can see a bridge.

As the bridge seems to speed toward the camera you can hear the other kid yelling, first a whoop of triumph, and the perspective of the camera changes as if he is actually standing up in the convertible. Then he sits back down quickly. Laughing. Then, "Whoa whoa, Graham, slow down! Jesus, slow down! Sl—"

The screen went black. My heart was racing. He'd kept footage of the crash where he'd lost his best friend. The last moments his friend had shot. I felt sick and did feel a wave of compassion for him. It was sad and strange and so quick. I was about to turn it off but then the screen lit again and it was additional footage, a slow pan of the whole wrecked car and the sound of whoever was holding the camera breathing heavily. Making impressed and incredulous terrified noises. Laughing. Crying. Then the camera rounds to the passenger side and you can see someone is lying on the hood of the car. His head is bleeding his face is bleeding the windshield has shattered and broken in half at his middle and cut into his stomach and there is glass and blood everywhere. I felt like I was going to throw up. I had never seen anything so terrible. A blood-spattered hand reaches down to touch the boy's head. And then he speaks and I was relieved! He was alive.

"Can you move?" Graham's voice asks.

The boy, Eric, smashed and mangled beyond recognition, looking barely human, moans.

Graham touches him again.

"Call nine-one-one," Eric gasps.

But the camera still focuses on his face. On his mouth which is full of blood. "Call nine-one-one," he says, and blood pours from his mouth and his ear.

The camera's perspective changes and you can see the boy's face full-on—his eyes open but unseeing, and then there is a moment where he suddenly sees Graham.

"Call nine-one-one," he says, his voice starting to rise in panic, his breath ragged as he begins to cry a little and then spits more blood onto the hood of the car. The camera stays focused on his face and the blood runs down the car and his face turns a white-gray and tears and blood run down his face. His eyes look into the camera pleading, then become vacant. After a few minutes his breathing becomes loud and labored, then his eyes go blank. It was the most horrible thing I had ever seen. The most terrible thing I can imagine anyone having to look at. That moment where his eyes became flat and empty.

But still the camera was running. There was nothing but the sound of the wind and some birds chirping. The boy's, Eric's, hair was partly matted with blood but the wind blew and tousled the part that wasn't. Then the camera changed perspective, panned back—Graham must have walked away a little and sat down—and you could see the whole front of the car and the dead boy on top of it. His broken body sliced by metal and glass and blood running everywhere.

You hear the scrape and click of a lighter being lit and you can hear Graham inhale, then exhale, then a cloud of gray smoke floats over the body of the boy. Graham was smoking. He was sitting beside the wreck with the camera trained on the last moments of his friend's life, casually smoking.

I don't know how long I sat there in his room. When I finally was aware of myself again, the front of my shirt was wet and I realized I had been crying. My hands were shaking. I didn't know what to do. I felt like I was outside my body, watching myself from the other side of the room.

Then finally I took the DVD out of the computer, put it into my pocket, and put the album cover back where I found it.

I had no idea when it was shot, but I was going to take it to the police right away.

ALLY

Syd came home so broken up and freaked-out I had no idea what could have happened to her. I thought at first she had been raped, it was that bad. She was shaking and crying. She told me she was going to report Graham to the police.

"What did he do to you?" I asked, angry and worried, grabbing her by the shoulders and looking into her face.

"Nothing," she said. "Nothing, it's what he did to you, and this movie he made of Eric."

"What movie?" I asked.

She went into our bathroom and threw up. I came in and held her hair back, then poured her a glass of water and sat on the side of the tub.

"Sis, what happened?"

"He has a movie of Eric dying," she said, and her voice had no emotion in it at all. "And he has films of you naked and talking about all kinds of things."

I could see she was terribly upset, but I knew Graham did not have movies of me naked and I knew there was no way he would take a video of his best friend dying. As far as I knew, Eric was still alive and Graham and I would go visit him on a road trip probably this coming summer. What I did see though was my sister losing her mind and I wanted to help her.

"What did the films look like?"

"OH!" she said. "And he has films of me, wearing your clothes. And I never wore your clothes or went sailing with our parents."

"He probably thought it was funny to make movies like that—just Photoshopped it."

"They weren't funny, they were creepy. They were all creepy."

"Come here," I said, and I put my arms around her. "Graham makes some weird movies and you might be upset about some of them, but I am sure they are either faked, like the ones of you, or just weird collage art. Think about it. You know Graham, you know how he is. Would he really do those things? I don't think so. You need to relax." She started crying. "Syd. Remember when you said we need to come together and be unified? We need to come together now. You need to relax. You need to take some of my optimism and see what has really happened instead of being stressed and hysterical about seeing some weird art."

"I have the movie here," she said, pulling it out of the pocket of her hoodie.

"Let me see it," I said.

"No, Ally. It will ruin your life. I'm taking it to the cops right now."

She looked determined and like that determination was the only thing that was keeping her going. But still. She might have something that could get Graham in trouble if it was taken out of context. "Give it to me, Syd!" I tried to grab it from her. "It's not ours. You've stolen it from his room. You shouldn't have been in his room."

She burst into tears, and pulled the disk close to her body, kicked at me with her feet. I hadn't ever seen her so upset— even when our parents would go away for whole days when we were little. I'd never seen her crying like that. "Get it through your head, Ally! He's bad. He's bad!" Her face was tear-streaked and swollen from crying. She looked desperate. There was nothing I could do. I had faith that she was wrong. I knew Graham wouldn't do anything to hurt me or hurt his friends. She was hysterical and there was no way I could protect her anymore. If she went to the police I was sure they would come to the same conclusion and send her home. In the end I had to let her go.

"Okay," I said. "Do what you have to do, sis. The police will decide if it's a problem or not. I can see how upset you are. Do it and then come home and I'll make you some hot cocoa. I'll bake you some muffins."

POLICE CHIEF BILL WERTZ

There was, of course, nothing we could do about the video he had. It was evidence from another crime, and he was apparently not using it for anything, just keeping it. The other videos she said he had we could never find, and sadly I think it was just something she made up so that there would be another reason to go after him.

We tried everything we could, called it a snuff film because that's essentially what it was, and that was all we could do. But you would be amazed at how wealth can tie up a court or how psychiatric experts can be used to turn things you know are wrong into things that are considered therapeutic. That family circled the wagons like nothing I'd ever seen in my life. Privilege doesn't begin to describe it. It was like we were nothing to them. They were some kind of royalty. The family's lawyer reminded the DA here repeatedly about double jeopardy. I don't know which was worse—them telling us that we'd victimized their son, or knowing that the kid's dad could just buy his freedom no matter what. And this came after everything that had happened to Brian.

We would sit around shaking our heads, wondering if this kid, Graham, was a sociopath, or if he was just the stupidest kid we'd ever come across. And then he would come in and be such a nice kid. I mean, polite, easygoing, incredibly relaxed, confident, focused. His parents clearly loved him and paid attention to him. He didn't look like he was capable of any of these things. And it really did remind you of why there's such a thing as juvenile detention—because kids don't think the same way as adults—some kids may never develop adult morals or understanding, some kids get more selfish as they get older, but most don't. Most people in Graham's situation would look back on his life and shudder. Know that they had made a mistake and wonder how they could even have been that person. That's the best you can hope for in a situation like that.

In the end the worst of it was how that girl got traumatized by seeing the video. I felt bad for her, I did. I can't imagine watching it and sitting right there in his room and knowing he was your friend. And of course it's bad having any kid learn the hard way that sometimes the justice system doesn't work like you want it to. Let alone a kid like Phil Tate's daughter. That girl did not listen to anyone and did not take no for an answer. She was a force. And after seeing that video, she was an unstoppable force.

SYD

felt like I was losing my mind. I went out and skated and skated and tried to get the images out of my head. I was so angry I thought I would burst. How could it be that I was the only one who saw how bad things were? I didn't tell anyone but the police about Graham's film. Of course I didn't tell my parents who probably didn't even notice I was upset at all. And when the police did nothing, I felt like my life was a puddle that was drying up. Everything seemed to get smaller and more terrifying.

How could what he had done be legal in any way? *How* could he hide who he was so easily? Why couldn't they just go into his house and grab the computer and arrest him and take him away? How could they tell me that I had been breaking and entering, committing a crime, when *he* was the one who was sick and dangerous?

I began having nightmares. Almost every night. We

were living right next door to this guy and still Ally slept soundly. She still didn't believe me but she was nicer to me than ever. We spent more time together. We would come home right after school and just sit in our room and talk. She knew something had happened, there's no way she didn't, but she still thought I was making up most of it or the police would have done something.

At some point, I felt so defeated I started believing her version of everything. It was easier just to believe her honestly, to deny everything I'd seen, to take comfort in her view of him. I let her take care of me, bake things. I just hung around the house with her. She still went out with Graham but I stayed home. I didn't feel like hanging out with my friends because I didn't want to burden them.

But one night everything shifted. Ally would tell me what Graham and she talked about sometimes, and he slipped up. She thought Eric was still alive and he told her he wanted her to come to Virginia with him and visit his grave.

Of course, she chalked it up to him "grieving," but I knew it was weirder than that. He told her he wanted her to come visit his grave and then the two of them would take a drive together on the roads that Eric and he used to drive in the Austin.

When she told me this, I got angry all over again. He wanted to do the same thing to Ally. He was looking for another Eric and he wasn't even being clever about it. He was so drug-addled and stupid and arrogant and he had no respect for my sister—he just told her like it was how he wanted to film her and kill her and she was still gullible enough to listen. He had said similar things to me. That's why he always wanted me to take his drugs.

He was looking for someone to take all the pills that make you brave and relaxed and think you're invincible and drive that person into a bridge or off a cliff or who knows what. And he didn't care if it was Ally or me or anyone. What he wanted was to see that image, to sell that image, to believe in the stupid idea that he was a cutting-edge artist doing things that no one could understand.

Then she told me the worst part. Every night she went over there he made another film of her. She was becoming his most popular subject, she said. His girl-next-door series. He said he wanted to have a thousand films of her. To film her her entire life.

I listened to Ally talk about Graham, saw the way she just believed everything he said. And I formulated my plan.

SYD

When I got home, Graham was standing on the roof of his garage looking out into the woods. He must have heard the skateboard because he turned around. Most of the town still thought he was a hero because of little Brian and even after the film emerged, his parents somehow made it look like he had kept this monstrosity of a movie because he loved his friend. I had never seen anything so sick. No one knew about that of course. Just me and him. And he didn't seem to care that I knew anymore. It had made him even more relaxed.

"Hey," he said. "I called you earlier but you didn't pick up."

I looked at my phone. There were no missed calls.

"Sure you didn't call Ally?"

He laughed. "Yeah, that must have been it. How's it going?"

I really couldn't believe that he could just talk so normally to everyone—considering all the secrets he had. But he was always like this. Gracious and charming when he was on the drugs, shy and polite when he wasn't. That's why it was so hard for people to believe what he was doing. Even when the evidence was staring them right in the face.

"It's good," I lied. "Hey, I was thinking about that thing you thought would be fun to do. I want to give the meds a try."

"Yeah?" he asked, raising his eyebrows. He hung off the side of the garage and then dropped to the driveway and walked over to me. "What part of it?"

"All of it," I said. "The driving, all of it. If we can drive with the top down."

I watched his breathing change and a smile spread across his face.

"It'll be fun," I said. "I want to feel how it feels. We can go after school on Thursday. We can drive up past the golf courses where there's no one around. I'll drive so you can film. Those drugs will make me a really good driver, right? The ones that make you focus?"

"Yeah," he said, looking deeply into my eyes. "They will. They'll make all of it so much better."

"Okay," I said, my heart pounding in my chest. He was so awful. And he had no trouble just going with me of course. He had no faithfulness or respect for my sister, would sell her out and cheat on her. He was the worst.

"Cool," he said. "I'm so happy we're going to do this. We're going to become immortal."

"Yeah, we're going to be stars," I said. "Hey, are you still selling those films?"

He nodded.

"The documentary ones of Ally?"

He nodded again and I thought, how could anyone be so stupid to admit that? He just knew he was bulletproof. He could admit to anything now, it didn't matter. He always got away with everything. Even if I deleted them, he would simply make more and keep posting them. I vowed that that would be the next part of my plan.

"It's an automatic system," he said. "I never shut it down."

"Can I be in some of them?" I asked.

He got that huge grin again. "Sure. Of course. We can make very different films than what me and Ally make."

"I want part of the money, though," I said.

He said, "You got it, partner. I'll see you Thursday at the old pier."

SYD

ALLY

GRAHAM

He was there standing out on the pier waiting for me. I flipped up my board and carried it while I walked along the wide wooden planks in the cold autumn air. My footsteps hollow, clunking along the dock. And then he turned and looked at me. He was beautiful. There was no denying it. I could see that his beauty was probably the thing that made his whole life possible. All the things he had done wrong all crimes all the "mistakes" forgiven when people looked into his pale-blue eyes and saw the smooth contours of his jaw. Or when they knew how much money his parents had. There was a light breeze and his T-shirt and thin jacket clung to him, showing the outline of his broad shoulders, his muscled form, his hair tousled and windblown.

"I'm so excited we're going to do this together," he said to me. Then he reached in his pocket and pulled out a little prescription bottle and rattled it. Smiled.

"What about our deal?" He nodded and reached in his jacket pocket, took out his keys—the key to the Austin, which had his house key attached—and handed them to me. As promised, he'd let me drive the Austin and in exchange he could film me doing it while on his special prescription.

"Thanks," I said, putting them in my pocket. I looked again at his beautiful face—the face that wasn't hiding anything evil—it was simply expressing nothing at all. He was like a big empty hole, someone built entirely of secondhand images of life and chemicals made to numb the experience of living it.

I smiled back at him and then took my skateboard in both hands, swung it fast like a bat and hit him in the face as hard as I could. There was a loud hollow sickening crack as he was knocked backward by the force of the blow and toppled into the water. The ocean was choppy and his body bobbed and drifted quickly north toward the yacht club. I looked down and saw the spray of blood across the pier and spattering my jacket. There was also blood on the board, but I would get rid of it in just a few minutes.

There. Done. Over. I turned to walk away, but gasped as Ally was literally right behind me—my face nearly touching her face. She was stunned and horror-stricken, in shock.

"What have you *done*?" she wailed, tears streaming down her face. "We have to get him out of the water, he's going to drown. He needs to go to a hospital!" She lunged for the water, but I held her back.

"No, Ally, we have to get out of here now. He hurt you. He hurt you and a lot of other people and he won't be able to do that anymore."

I held her around the waist and pulled her backward into my arms, trying to drag her off the dock as she dug in her heels. Finally she broke free and ran, threw herself off the end of the dock into the water with him.

"Ally, stop. *Stop!* There's nothing we can do now. This was his fate. This is how it ends for him after all the things he did."

I saw her struggling in the water. Ally is a great swimmer. She had lifted his head above the water, his face torn and bruised and broken, his nose flattened his lips smashed. She was swimming with one arm around him making slow progress to the ladder beneath the dock.

"Let him go, Ally, we have to get out of here. Let him go," I said. "I won't let you bring him back up on this dock."

It seemed that he was still breathing—bubbles of foamy blood came out of his mouth and nose. His weight was pulling Ally down. I watched my sister struggling, crying flailing in the water, trying desperately to carry the weight of someone who was more than half dead, who had filmed her naked and lied to her and sold her image to old men who wanted to do her harm, someone who did this all under the guise of loving her. I couldn't bear to see her this way. And I knew I would almost rather see her dead than see her revive Graham Copeland.

Almost.

"Help me get him up the ladder," she called to me, spitting water from her mouth and gasping.

"No," I said.

"Sydney! Please, we can't do this. Please! Help me!" She inhaled water and then spluttered and choked it up. Her head disappearing below the surface for a minute. I climbed down the ladder and kicked hard at his body to get it away from her, but she held tightly to him. I am certain he was already dead but still she clung to him, trying to raise his face, putting his body above hers.

I grabbed the ladder with one hand, then held tight to her wrist with the other and put my foot on Graham's shoulder, trying to sink him back beneath the waves as I pulled her up.

She was crying hysterically and shouting for me to stop and then I watched it happen. A large wave came cresting in and threw her against the base of the peer knocking her unconscious. It pulled her down where I couldn't see her anymore. And only Graham's body was bobbing there streaming blood.

I felt light-headed. I screamed her name and dove into the cold waves. I swam in the choppy water trying to see her. I thrashed in the water in my soaking cumbersome clothes for what seemed like an eternity. Minutes ticked by, each second a precious moment of my sister's life. Then I caught a glimpse of her floating facedown far away—the wave that had crested had sucked her right out into the harbor. She wasn't moving.

I knew that she was dead and that the water was already freezing my limbs making it impossible for me to swim. I climbed back up the ladder and raced to Graham's car, looking for a cell phone or anything I could call someone from. There was nothing. I screamed for help but the whole idea of meeting at the abandoned pier is that there is no one to help. I looked for a rope I could throw to her—knowing as the minutes raced by that there was no way she could have survived this.

I heard myself scream as if I were drowning and then I ran. Fast. I had to save the only thing I could.

I put the key in the ignition, turned the car around and drove frantically to Graham's house. His parents were not home—and if mine were they didn't notice their dripping-wet daughter crying and whimpering as she fumbled for the neighbor's house key and let herself in.

I raced up to his room and followed the instructions Becky had given me and got to the dummy site—logged in and then there it was. The swirling beach-ball timer showing how many girl-next-door videos were being downloaded.

I logged into Graham's site administrator page and voided the sale of the videos. Then I called up the full list of other footage, selected them all, and hit delete. I knew I was destroying evidence. But the boy who had committed that crime had already paid. And so had my sister. I would not let him be the one who controlled what people remembered of her. I would not have people know her for anything other than what she really was. Not a piece of meat, or some girl who should have known better, or all the other terrible things people say about girls when boys hurt them and use them. I had gotten rid of all the disgusting images he made of people because he thought that they weren't real or were just for his own entertainment or his own way to make money.

When I got back to the pier, their waterlogged forms still bobbed in the waves and I was wracked with guilt. I had made sure Ally's life would speak for itself. But she was still gone.

It didn't seem possible. I'd tried to save her, and now she was floating below me in the harbor she'd loved, beside the boy she never should have loved. I couldn't let her drift anymore. I dove into the icy waves to drag her out, pull her up the ladder, to feel her hand in mine one last time. And I rocked in the waves, swimming with her head against my chest, clinging to my sister's body as if it were my own.

POLICE CHIEF BILL WERTZ

We still don't know exactly what happened. It seemed they fell in together. Or might have been attacked by a third party, who we haven't yet found. Both of their faces were smashed. One from a flat, blunt object, the other from the pier. They died maybe ten minutes apart.

The strangest part was the boy's home.

His bedroom was covered with puddles of ocean water, his computer equipment partly wrecked, all his files destroyed, sometime after the accident. His car seat was soaking wet, but the car was still parked where he left it by the pier. And no fingerprints anywhere. Not one.

We questioned Becky and Declan, but they hadn't seen Phil Tate's daughter in over a week before it happened. She'd been staying home. We talked to the parents and they said the same. The girl seemed preoccupied but fine.

We don't know what we are looking at here. We don't

know if this is a murder or a double suicide or a jealous fight that got out of hand. There are only two bodies. Two kids that lived next door to each other.

We do know that Graham Copeland found trouble wherever he went and that this time trouble found him.

Rockland Mourns the Loss of National Merit Scholar, Avid Sailor

Allyson Sydney Tate (1998–2015)

Allyson Sydney Tate died last week in a marina accident. "Tate," as she was known to her friends, family, and teachers, was to be the valedictorian of her class. She worked for a year at the Pine Grove Inn, sailed with her father, skateboarded, and sold muffins at fund-raisers for the Rockland Historical Society. She won several science fairs for Rockland High School, but most people remember Sydney for her exuberant spirit, quick wit, keen ability to debate, and her love of skateboarding. She could always be seen doing tricks at the skate park on a board she built herself. Sydney was known for her independence, her stylish flair, and her love for punk-rock music. Her dream was to go to Stanford with her friend, class salutatorian Declan Wells, and study chemistry. Calling hours are Tuesday 6–8 p.m. at Shady Point Methodist Church. In lieu of flowers donations can be made to the Tony Hawk Foundation, which builds skate parks in urban areas and helps keep neglected kids out of trouble.

ACKNOWLEDGMENTS

I am extremely grateful to my agent Rebecca Friedman for her friendship, intelligence, and insight. She has made this book possible. My editor, Claudia Gable, is a superhero. Her integrity, creativity, and intellect have helped guide this book from idea to reality and I'm lucky to have the opportunity to work with her. I'm also tremendously thankful to Katherine Tegen for her genius and vision; so proud to be a part of her list. Melissa Miller, Alexandra Arnold, and the whole team at Katherine Tegen Books are talented and dedicated people. What a pleasure it is to write among such company.